DEROS Vietnam:

Dispatches from the Air-Conditioned Jungle

Doug Bradley

The more common experience of war in all branches of the service is that of support. Bullets, beans, and bandages don't get to the grunts by magic. Doug Bradley's stories explore the Vietnam War as experienced by the majority of its veterans. These stories are not about battle, but like all great stories they are about the battle for the human soul. Bradley is a talented and experienced writer and he describes that battle with clarity, insight, humor, and great skill.

Karl Marlantes, author of *Matterhorn: A Novel of the Vietnam War*

In prose that is adamantly stark and spare, Doug Bradley shares this impressive collection of stories loosely centered around the rarely told experience of those American vets who served in Vietnam in the rear. That he is able to pack so much punch, emotions and poignancy in short stories that are tightly woven and compact is a true testament to his gift as a writer and storyteller.

Lan Cao, author of *Monkey Bridge*

The best stories often come late. These DEROS stories from Doug Bradley, a Vietnam scholar who served there more than four decades ago, are among the best I've read. Each story is clear and clean and evocative, looking at the experience from a slightly different angle. The full effect provides a fearful symmetry.

David Maraniss, author of *They Marched into Sunlight*

DEROS Vietnam:

Dispatches from the Air-Conditioned Jungle

Doug Bradley

WARRIORS PUBLISHING GROUP

NORTH HILLS, CALIFORNIA

DEROS Vietnam: Dispatches from the Air-Conditioned Jungle

A Warriors Publishing Group book/published by arrangement with the author.

PRINTING HISTORY
Warriors Publishing Group edition/November 2012

ISBN 978-0-9853388-1-7

10 9 8 7 6 5 4 3 2 1

To all those who served in Vietnam but didn't
live to see their DEROS date.

Introduction:
The Air-Conditioned War

I spent 365 days in Vietnam from November of 1970 to November of 1971. I worked in a corporate-esque, shine and polish, public information office in the U.S. Army's headquarters at Long Binh, a former rubber plantation about 15 miles from Saigon. How in the hell I ended up there after my graduation from college in May 1969 and not at law school at Boston University where I'd been accepted is a question I still ask myself.

And while I think the answer has something to do with Nixon, the draft, Vietnamization, my birthday, and bad luck, I've more or less given up trying to figure it out. The reality is I didn't go to law school and I did get drafted. Vietnam became my real graduate school—my true education if you will—and it's something that continues to teach me a lesson every day of my life.

My Long Binh officemates and I were categorized as REMFs: Rear Echelon Mother Fuckers. That was meant, I believe, to distinguish us from the grunts, the guys who were fighting the war, but I also think it was meant to keep us in our place, and to be a slap in the face. As far as I can tell, it worked. We were less than the grunts, and we still feel guilty about having a safer, cushier job than our brothers who did the fighting and dying.

That doesn't mean there wasn't any pain and sacrifice and danger for us REMFs. But it's muted, much like our collective Vietnam voice, because, well, most of what we did wasn't glorious or heroic or even very interesting. Trying to unmute that REMF voice is part of the reason why I've been writing about Vietnam for more than 40 years. I mean, hell, there were more of us in the rear than there were grunts in the field, and we did have to put up with all the military and political and Vietnam bullshit too, so why doesn't anybody know about our experiences?

Truth is, that's way too noble a motivation for me and this collection of stories. I wrote them mainly for myself because the process of writing has helped me to better understand Vietnam—and to heal myself a little in the process. I need to write, I have to write, to be who I am. There's as much of the non-Vietnam me in here as there is the Vietnam me.

But I doubt you'll be able to tell the difference.

There is some truth to the Nixon-draft-Vietnamization-birthday-bad-luck mantra I mentioned earlier. For starters, I blame all U.S. presidents from FDR on for getting us into Vietnam. But up until Spring 1968, my junior year in college, I figured if I stayed in school long enough and got my college diploma, the war would be over. I mistakenly believed Lyndon Baines Johnson. I wouldn't make the same mistake with the next president.

I sure as hell didn't buy Tricky Dick's B.S. about a "secret plan to win the war" and all that. I was so pissed at LBJ that I projected my anger on to his V.P., Hubert H. Humphrey. In the end, I marked my virgin trip to the ballot box on November 5, 1968 by writing in Dick Gregory for president. That's the only vote I ever cast—and I've voted in every election since—that I wish I had back.

Not long after Nixon ascended to the throne in 1969, I began to pay more attention to what was going on with the war and the draft. LBJ had cancelled graduate school deferments in March 1968, so even with my law school acceptance at B.U. later, military conscription appeared more likely than law school matriculation.

On a beautiful spring day in 1969, I graduated from tiny Bethany College in Bethany, West Virginia. It was May 24 to be exact, and while Led Zeppelin brought down the house that night with "Dazed and Confused" at the Kinetic Playground in Chicago and the Grateful Dead jammed to "Going Down the Road Feeling Bad" at Seminole Indian Village in Florida, my parents drove me back to Philadelphia in their tiny red VW.

Thus began the worst summer of my life.

I was now classified 1-A (available for unrestricted military service) as opposed to 2-S (deferred because of collegiate study). Every day brought the same throbbing headache, the crippling knot in the stomach, and the perpetual conundrum: *What in the hell am I going to do?*

I'll admit I let the trauma and the anxiety and the fear get the best of me. I ballooned to well over 190 pounds (I've weighed around 160 ever since Vietnam), pissed and moaned all summer long, and turned down a couple decent jobs. I ended up working in a tiny factory where they made locks for aircraft carriers. I increased my intake of alcohol and marijuana. I was lonely and miserable.

I wasn't eager to give more than two years of my life away to the Army—or the Navy, Marines, or Air Force—and I didn't have any pull to help me get into the National Guard or Reserves. That seemed like a major copout anyway.

So, I sat and ate and smoked and cursed and waited.

September 1969 eventually rolled around. *Vietnamization*—a term coined by Melvin Laird, a

Wisconsinite and Secretary of Defense—was sailing along, but there were still nearly a half million of my peers in Viet-nam. It was just a matter of time until the draft caught up with me, so I dropped out of law school and dropped into my pre-induction physical for the draft. It was like a never-ending episode of "The Twilight Zone," and I kept hearing Rod Serling's smoky voice warning me: *This highway leads to the shadowy tip of reality: you're on a through route to the land of the different, the bizarre, the unexplainable. . .* By the time I came to, I'd passed with flying colors. I was on my way to the land of the different.

Which is exactly where luck, good and bad, and birthdays intervened. To show the American public that Vietnamization was working, Nixon boldly cancelled November and December draft calls, so guys like me could worry about their uncertain futures a little longer. He then introduced a "more just and equitable means" for conscription—the lottery.

In this case, having the winning number was not what you wanted. No, you wanted to lose the lottery so you could keep your ass out of Vietnam.

On December 1, 1969, at Selective Service National Headquarters in Washington, D.C., 366 blue plastic capsules, each containing a day of the year, were placed in a large glass jar and drawn by hand to assign order-of-call numbers to all American males between the ages of 18 and 26. It was just and equitable all right, but for those of us with our lives hanging in the balance, it was the ultimate horror show, a real game of Russian roulette, not the bogus crap Michael Cimino later invented in "The Deer Hunter." Except this time the lone bullet rotated among 366 chambers.

It was also one of the bigger media events of the year. All the TV networks were there—we only had four back then—and radio and film, too, as well as newspapers and wire service reporters and Congressional types and on and on. It definitely was a circus, but with the feel of a public hanging lingering in the air.

I chose to listen to the lottery on the radio in a Philadelphia suburb, playing cards and drinking beer with my brother and sister-in-law, rather than watch with my parents, who were even more uptight about all this than I was. I knew I wouldn't be able to handle their stress as well as mine. So, I more or less listened to the goings-on and got really drunk.

The first capsule, drawn by a Republican Congressman from New York who served on the House Armed Services Committee, contained the date September 14. The last one drawn was June 8—the day after my June 7 birthday, which came in at 85, eventually landing me in Fort Dix, New Jersey by March and Vietnam that following November.

Now that my fate was more or less determined, I devoted more time to feeling sorry for myself—and to being pissed at my parents since they were the ones responsible for my June 7 birthday. What if they'd waited to have sex? What if my dad hadn't arrived back home from the war horny and eager to affirm his survival? What if my mom could have endured a few more hours of labor? What if she didn't have to have a C-section, which the hospital probably wouldn't have accommodated the next day, a Sunday? What if . . .

That perverse line of inquiry was my only holdover from my flirtation with law school. Now that I was a marked man, I didn't know how long I had until my blindfold and last cigarette, so I left the country right after New Year's Day. Not for exile in Canada, where it was cold and protected, but for a respite in a tropical paradise like Nassau in the Bahamas, where the U.S. had jurisdiction. Let them come after me, I muttered to myself, armed every day with a book, some ganja and a gin and tonic.

They never came.

It took being away from the USA for me to realize just how much I'd been missing during my period of self-absorption. Two big anti-war moratoria, My Lai, murders and mayhem, the Bahamian locals and travelling beach bums knew about all this and more, and I'd listen to their conversations deep into the night before I'd stumble back to my beach bungalow for another round of self-pity.

Some time during that trip, I sobered up long enough to fall in love with Christine from Buffalo, a wandering romantic like myself who loved F. Scott Fitzgerald and Rod McKuen and saw the world through rose-colored glasses, literally. I took the fact that Christ was in her name as a sign that I'd be saved.

It didn't happen.

After Christine headed back to college in Buffalo and I ran out of money, I made a decision about my future. Among my three shitty options—jail, Canada or the military—I chose Door Number Three. Where was Monty Hall when I needed him?

Arriving "back in the USSR" in February 1970, I was welcomed by an inviting letter from Uncle Sam that proclaimed "Greetings!" Four weeks later, on March 2, 1970, I raised my hand and swore an oath to God and country along with a hundred or so like-minded sheep in a U.S. Army induction center in Pittsburgh, Pennsylvania. Why Pittsburgh and not Philadelphia where I was currently living? That's because Pittsburgh is where I registered for the draft and that's where my Selective Service board was located.

This is where luck, good and bad, and fate and timing and whatever else you want to call it began to intervene, or at least I began to notice the intervention. Like many baby boomers, I'd figured that what separated us as soldiers—later veterans—from reservists and protestors and MIAs and deserters and POWs and draft avoiders came down to luck, fate and timing—who you knew, where you lived, when you graduated from high school, how you were raised, how many WWII movies you saw, when you turned 18, whether or not you committed a crime, big or small, at 17 or 18, when your number came up, etc. etc.

Hell, for me, even the fact that I turned 18 in Pittsburgh, thereby registering for selective service in that blue collar city, but was back living in Philadelphia at age 22 when I got drafted—meaning I boarded a bus in Philly in the wee hours of March 2 and headed west to the Steel City to take my vows with Uncle Sam—had everything to do with my eventually being assigned to Fort Dix, New Jersey and not Fort Bragg, North Carolina for basic training. Everything changed with that simple twist of fate.

Similarly, prior to my rendezvous with Uncle Sam in Pittsburgh, I'd serendipitously sat beside a soldier on a late February flight to Buffalo to visit Christine. Even though I did everything I could to avoid sitting next to this guy (back in those days, folks with student IDs and guys in the military both flew "stand by" on planes so the two of us were called up to the podium just before takeoff and were seated next to each other), we eventually struck up a conversation that would have a direct impact on my Army career.

"By the end of the first couple days of basic training," the helpful GI told me, "you're going to be totally frazzled, and really pissed." Even though this guy looked younger than I was, there was something in his eyes and in his voice that made him a lot older. "Then they lay on you a battery of aptitude tests and other shit. Don't blow these off," he raised his voice and pinned my wrist to the arm rest. I jumped.

"When you get in there, be awake, be serious. Take the tests seriously because they might help you get a good MOS."

I knew this was important, but what the hell was an MOS?

"MOS is your military job," he continued, "it stands for Military Occupational Specialty. Mine was 25C40, radio operator. Those tests that you don't want to take and are pissing you off go a long way to deciding what the Army wants to do with you." He stared so hard into my eyes that I thought he could see my soul, my fear.

"Even if you're drafted?" I asked, barely audible. I figured my ass was grass because of the draft.

"Yeah, even if you're drafted," he said. My spirits lifted. "I was drafted," he went on, "but they sent me to radio training after basic. Not everybody who gets drafted goes to combat." He paused. "Of course, there are no guarantees."

There was yet another of the Vietnam-era mantras. "No guarantees." Of safety, of sanity, of being whole, of getting laid. Of coming back. No guarantees.

No shit.

The soldier on the plane to Buffalo was right. And I thank him wherever he is because his unsolicited advice helped me nail those basic aptitude tests and be expertly prepared for a follow-up interview so that the Army awarded me an MOS of 71Q20—Information Specialist—at the end of basic training. I was going to be an Army journalist. Or was that an oxymoron?

Of course that knowledge didn't come until after eight weeks of worry and fear and harassment. The drill sergeants at Ft. Dix knew I was a college grad, one of only two in my basic training platoon, and they bugged me relentlessly every day about becoming an officer instead of a grunt.

"Bradley, you're a smart guy, a college boy," they'd tease me, "so why don't you save your sorry ass and sign up for OCS (Officer Candidate School)? Officers give orders and have cushy jobs. You don't want to be the guy taking the orders, especially if you're a grunt," they'd snarl. "And as sure as I'm Ho Chi Minh, the Army will make you a grunt and you'll be DOA if you don't sign up for OCS!"

Sure, I was scared. But not scared enough to become a "shake and bake," a.k.a. second lieutenant. Even though I was new to the Army, I already understood that being a junior officer in Vietnam might lead to a one-way ticket. So, I kept my head down, kept my mouth shut, and humped my ass through eight weeks of basic training.

Because my defenses were up and my anxiety high, I didn't take the time to make deep connections with the other guys in my platoon. Those two months are like an old kinescope of faces, places, and nerves. Of Baby Fat Bob singing "Fire and Rain" every morning before formation, of black Murphy from Brooklyn saying he was going to knife me and white Murphy from New Jersey saying he'd get the other Murphy back, of two trips to the Big Apple with Billy and Doc and Four Eyes and Rufus to see Chris and her crazy, oversexed girlfriends from her all-girls school in Buffalo. Of mud and rain and night infiltration and weapons familiarization. And a somber Easter dinner with my parents at the Ft. Dix PX. I was the Pascal lamb, and there wasn't a resurrection in my horoscope.

There was also a visit to the base chaplain to inquire about Conscientious Objector status and long talks with my drill sergeant about bravery and cowardice and picking up a gun.

Right before we completed Basic Training, Nixon announced his decision to launch American forces into Cambodia. I remember a bunch of us standing around one of the sergeant's rooms watching a black and white TV on April 30 as Nixon pointed at maps and said things like "it is not our power but our will and character that is being tested tonight" and "the time has come for action."

The drill sergeants who'd been over there were shaking their heads and twirling their dog tags. The rest of us were clueless as to what was going on, but that didn't prevent us from joining in the litany of fuck, fuckin' A, fucked up, fuckin', fubar, and other declensions of the GI's favorite word.

Later that night it started to sink in. The goddamn war wasn't cooling down, it was heating up. The odds of us draftees becoming grunts had just gotten a whole lot worse.

And the next day was May Day. How goddamn appropriate that was, since we'd be getting our MOSs and shipped to our next assignments.

The tension in the barracks the following morning was off the charts. No one spoke as we showered and dressed and prepared to meet our maker. Ours was one of several companies preparing to graduate from basic training on a perfect spring day. Our drill sergeants approached, accompanied by a handful of guys who looked like junior accountants. I couldn't hear what they were saying until Flipper (he had big ears) turned to me and hollered: "Brads, they want you."

Time stopped. My heart was pounding so hard that I couldn't hear what the Spec. 4 accountant-type was saying. I followed him into a building and stood in a small line, as he directed. By the time I got to the front of the line, I was ready to piss my pants. Had the drill sergeants signed me up for OCS after all? Could they do that? Was I going to have to take basic training over because I'd paid somebody to cover my last KP? Did they know I was smoking marijuana? It hit me at that moment that I had no control whatsoever over what the Army wanted to do with me. Just put me on a plane to Vietnam now. I was fucked.

"Private Bradley!" The young soldier behind the glass was trying to get my attention. "These are your orders and this is the voucher you use for your plane fare." He handed me a bunch of official-looking papers and, without even looking me in the eye, shouted "Next."

My hands were shaking as I glanced down at my orders. I quickly cut through all the military folderol to realize two things: I was going to have a 10-day leave, and I was to report to the Army Hometown News Center in Kansas City on Tuesday, May 12.

Holy shit! I wasn't going to Advanced Infantry Training. I wasn't a grunt, and maybe I wasn't even going to Vietnam. I almost kissed the guy standing in line behind me. I was overjoyed.

But my joy was short-lived, because as I headed back to formation, the eyes of every guy in my platoon were on me, wondering *What happened? You okay?* I nodded, tried not to smile, and stood there with them as they received their orders to Ft. Polk, Ft. Sill, Ft. Benning. They were all boarding trains heading south that night. Most of them would be in Vietnam by the fall.

I never heard from any of those guys, and while I can still see their faces, especially as they were on that sunny day in May, I don't remember their names. It's just as well because I'd be afraid I'd find too many of them etched in black granite on The Wall.

Kent State erupted the following Monday, May 4. Every time the phone rang or there was a knock on my parents' apartment door during my leave, I figured it was the Army telling me to grab a gun and go shoot some students. I was convinced that I'd be taking up weapons against my peers before I'd have to shoot a Viet Cong.

I spent much of that ten days in Buffalo with Christine, trying to decide if the revolution was underway or whether I should go to Canada. We went to the movies instead and sat through "Z" a couple times, our mouths agape. Fiction and reality had become one and the same, and we both felt as if what was happening in a celluloid Greece was happening in Vietnam and Ohio and Jackson, Mississippi. I was almost relieved to put on my uniform and get the hell to Kansas City. It somehow seemed safer.

The Army Hometown News Center was located on Troost Avenue in Kansas City, the same street where Walt Disney had his first studio. The irony was not lost on me as we pretended to share good news with parents and loved ones across the USA about their sons who were far away in Vietnam. We never talked about the deaths, and we never wrote about them either.

It was a long, hot summer and I allowed myself to join the other lotus-eaters, acting as if the war in Vietnam and the one in America weren't happening. Christine paid a couple visits, I shared a decent apartment with two GI roommates, and there wasn't any extra duty to pull since we lived in a city and not on a base. I had to admit that Army life was pretty good.

The very best thing about Kansas City was meeting George, who became my best friend and lifelong confidant. He struck me as the complete antithesis of a soldier—skinny, brainy, and a daddy. We lived together the first couple weeks before his wife and baby daughter joined him from D. C. I couldn't understand why the Army would pursue a guy like George, but of course logic and good decision-making had nothing to do with this shit show.

Everything was going good, too good, until a late July morning when George and I were summoned into the Master Sergeant's office. He told us that we'd just come down on levy to go to Vietnam. I never understood the levy concept, but it had something to do with big-ass IBM computers at the Pentagon that had punch cards with all our names and MOS and dates, etc., so that when somebody with your MOS left Vietnam, they ran the computer to identify who was out there to replace them. It reeked of Robert McNamara's—he was both JFK and LBJ's defense secretary—brand of troop management by machine.

Unfortunately for me and George, our punch cards were in the database and our numbers came up that day. We were to report to Travis Air Base north of San

Francisco on November 4 for our tour of duty in Vi-etnam.

I was surprised by how unprepared I was for this terrible news. I spent the first few days on the phone with Chris, who was making contacts with the Underground Railroad types in Canada. "You can't go to Vietnam." She sounded pretty adamant. "You can't."

But I did. Sure I agonized and second-guessed and even entertained the Canada scenario briefly, but in the end I upped my intake of booze and dope and partied my way out of Kansas City and back to Philadelphia for a 30-day leave.

That was the lowest of the lows. I couldn't look my parents in the eye, especially my mom, who teared up every time we exchanged a glance. My dad was in pain, too, but he didn't know how to deal with it, so he took me and my brother to watch a prize fight which I guess made him feel better.

I spent nearly two of the weeks in Buffalo and that was no picnic either. Neither Christine nor I would talk about that sword of Damocles hanging over my head, but we sure as hell were thinking about it. We stayed away from other conversations too, including the obligatory one of who would wait for whom and how true we'd be to one another. We mostly sat around her house listening to Laura Nyro albums.

I grew enormously sick and tired of all the people who shook my hand or patted me on the back or gave me a hug and wished me well and told me I was a hero and thanked me for what I was about to do. None of them believed how badly I didn't want to do this. Why weren't they listening? Why weren't they helping?

By day 30, I'd made some peace with myself and my parents. I didn't marry Chris. And I met George in San Francisco on November 4.

George and I got split up early on. He was up, up and away to Vietnam while I had to wait several more days for my death warrant. I spent those days donating blood so I'd be relieved of extra duties and reading James Joyce's *Ulysses* in the base library. I nearly became invisible.

The orders came. They always do. I boarded a plane late on November 10, stopped in Alaska and Japan, crossed the International Date Line, and arrived at the 90th Replacement Battalion in Long Binh on November 12. Then another of those fate-timing-luck moments occurred as I ended up being sent just a few clicks from where I was standing, to the Information Office at USARV Headquarters in the same exact office where George was working. I was safe and I was alive.

And I intended to keep it that way.

Long Binh was a major supply area and headquarters base. It was bigger than big. And it was a sanctuary for pencil-pushers like me and my officemates, as well as legions of clerks, logistics specialists, attaché aides, and others lucky enough to escape field duty. If it came down to a battle of rulers and pens and compasses, I was certain we'd get the best of the Viet Cong and North Vietnamese. But that wasn't the war we were fighting.

In fact, for most of my time in country, we weren't fighting at all. With Vietnamization and the expanded air war and the renewed peace talks, there was an atmosphere of *I sure as hell ain't gonna be the last GI killed in Vietnam* about everything. Disagreements and defiance were daily occurrences. Hair was long, tempers were short, stimulants were plentiful, and the racial and generational divides were deep and growing. Huge.

I remember things getting hairy just twice—once during the invasion of Laos in February, 1971 and the other during the South Vietnamese so-called elections for president in August later that year. Both times Long Binh post was on red alert as we office-types stumbled and bumbled our way out to bunker line. I doubt we could have held off anybody, but lucky for us we didn't have to.

Such relative tranquility in no way diminished the fighting and dying still occurring almost daily. Thousands of my brothers were killed while I was there. Although I was a correspondent, I reported none of those deaths. The feel, the vibe of Vietnam in 1971 was to keep your head down, look out for one another, find a way to get through the day, fuck the lifers.

At the USARV Information Office (IO), we worked 11 hour-days, six days a week. Thanks to the high-priced help we worked for, our offices were comfortably air-conditioned. And except for the lifers who ordered us around, almost everybody in the IO office was a college grad like George and me. My alma mater, Bethany College, was the least impressive among a pedigree that included Boston College, NYU, Berkeley, and the University of Wisconsin. Maybe that's why we read a lot of books, debated the vagaries of the American popular TV shows they broadcast on the Armed Forces Vietnam Network, or AFVN, and played a highly intellectual game of 20 questions we called Botticelli.

We lived better than most, spending our down time in hooches, two of us to a tiny cubicle with two bunks, two lockers, electric fans, and Vietnamese *mama-san* housemaids who cleaned, made our beds, shined our shoes, did our laundry, and every now and then helped us buy contraband on the black market.

There was a bar in front of our hooch with a big refrigerator and a chalk board that listed the names of those whose job it was to buy the beer for that month at the PX. Hard liquor and cognac—extremely popular on the Vietnamese black market—were also available for PX purchase. Everybody smoked cigarettes, most smoked Mary Jane, and everything was cheap, including lives.

It obviously could have been a lot worse, and we saw some of that on the days we went back and forth to Saigon to assemble or mail our office newspaper, the *Army Reporter*, and especially saw it when we were sent to cover a story beyond the Long Binh confines. One of the best reporters in our office, Steve Warner, was killed during the invasion of Laos.

So, try as we did, we weren't immune from the war. We just never wrote about it that way. Our way was always how we were winning the hearts and minds of the Vietnamese, or how we were handing the war over to them, even though the real picture was a lot different. That's not a roll of film we'd ever expose. And we underlings couldn't risk pissing off Uncle Sam and getting our asses sent to the DMZ.

There was a lot of country, and a nation full of people, between Long Binh and the DMZ, but we never took the time to get to know that or them either. We never saw the country as a country but solely as a war. We only saw the Vietnamese through that prism, too— the alien enemy, maids, bar girls, pimps, prostitutes, slaves, and servants. No wonder the Vietnamese call this the *American War* and not the *Vietnam War*.

As I look back on it now, I realize that Vietnam was a little like Kansas City in terms of my state of amnesia. I worked, ate, slept, smoked, drank, laughed, read, joked, and pretended that my other, "real" life was still moving along somewhere. The fact that I was in the rear, that I wasn't in kill-or-be-killed situations, and that this was 1971 and not 1968 helped lull me to sleep. In some ways, it's taken me this long to wake up, but not soon enough to save a generation from Iraq and Afghanistan.

Most everything else about that time and those people is in these stories, with the requisite names changed to protect the innocent—and the guilty. Between each of the longer stories I've placed an interlinear piece—what Ernest Hemingway referred to as an "interchapter" in his classic World War I work *In Our Time*. These very short pieces serve as a magnifying glass to focus attention on an aspect from its related, longer story.

Short or long, writing these pieces has pushed me, after all these years, to complete my own cycle. Some is eerily autobiographical, some fictional, and some a little of both. What it all means and how much it matters is now up to you.

Table of Contents

Dog Tags

Everybody said the reason Murphy tried to frag Lieutenant Colonel Fraser was because of the chewing out and the court-martial. They talked about how Fraser's face got right up next to Murphy's the morning after Steve Ward's DEROS party and how it changed colors when he let Murphy have it. Everyone agreed: that incident was what damn near did in the old Lt. Col.

I know different. I know because I dropped by Long Binh Jail during my last day off and got the real lowdown straight from the mouth of Private Dwayne Murphy. He didn't try to off Fraser because of the ass chewing or the extra duty the Lt. Col. gave us for the bathroom graffiti. It wasn't the curfew restrictions or even how he busted Murphy with a court-martial after Ward's DEROS party.

"It was the dogs," Murphy told me. Everybody forgot about the goddamn dogs.

"He was fucking crazy," he explained to me and the darkness. "Out of control."

The two of us sat with a large black MP between us in the bowels of LBJ, Long Binh Jail, thousands of miles from our former lives back home.

"Every fucking thing he did was part of some weird master plan, just like this goddamn war. All Fraser and the rest of the brass understand is winning, getting ahead. They don't know a goddamn thing about life. Only death." He paused. "When he told us to kill the goddamn dogs, I knew that was it. He had to be stopped."

Things had been strange around our office ever since Colonel Brock left a few months before the shit went down. Back then, our IO unit ran like a well-oiled machine—we ground out the weekly newspaper, press releases, hometown tapes, and public and command information, all without a hitch. Not a week went by without the tiny, bald Brock strutting into our office, smiling around the room and congratulating everyone within earshot: "Damn fine newspaper this week! Damn fine paper!" He made us feel good about the jobs we were doing, even if we were in the Army.

Then Brock's tour was up and he headed back to the world. And Lt. Col. Walter Fraser arrived. It was like the air had gone out of our balloon and we'd landed smack dab in Vietnam. Things changed for all of us, but especially Murphy. He and Col. Brock were tight. They'd spent some time together stateside—attended the same university before 'Nam. Everyone had their own version of the story about the savvy, fatherly colonel and the eccentric freshman from Minneapolis together at the radical hotbed University of Wisconsin.

I'd never been anywhere near the Midwest, never been to college, but I'd heard about the riots and anti-war activity. And right there in the midst of it all was good old Colonel Brock. A helluva place for an Army lifer, but that was the kind of guy Brock was. Hippies, teargas and all, he had Uncle Sam send him to Wisconsin to study public relations. Damned if he and Murphy didn't end up taking some of the same classes!

By the time I'd been in 'Nam long enough to know my ass from a hole in the ground, the Brock-Murphy bond was common knowledge. Every time we had a DEROS party or holiday bash, somebody would egg them on to talk about their "student radical days" together in Madison.

There was a lot of good-natured joking and some intense political discussion—Murphy didn't buy into Brock's analysis of Ho Chi Minh's propaganda strategy; Brock thought Murphy's capitalist theory of Southeast Asian exploitation was naïve—but Murphy and the Colonel shared a real affection. They might have held very different ideas about the Army and the war, but they had a helluva lot of respect for each other. You couldn't miss it.

So, when they transferred the old man to the Army War College to teach the art of military propaganda or some shit, Murphy missed him way more than the rest of us. It seemed like part of him left. Maybe if they hadn't been so close, Murphy might have been better able to deal with Lt. Col. Fraser.

So much has changed. Since Fraser took over, the paper's gone to hell, guys have gotten transferred or reassigned, half the old gang's DEROS-ed, and their replacements don't know shit. Makes it pretty tough for us short timers.

We figured we were in for it even before Fraser arrived. Sgt. First Class Kennedy had given us a background briefing, and it wasn't pretty. Fraser didn't have any journalism or information training; he'd never been near an IO office during his two decades in the Army. In the last six months he'd jumped from Da Nang to Quang Ngai to Soc Trang. It seems he was obsessed with earning a Legion of Merit citation and his colonel's silver eagle. Even Kennedy, who prided himself on his commitment to military command and control, was a little apprehensive. Brock's laid-back policies made his job easier since we all behaved ourselves and he didn't have to get on our case.

For the first couple of days, Fraser faked us out. Somebody must have tipped him off because he came on kinda low key and friendly. But it didn't take long for his true character to assert itself. It all started on a fateful Friday—July 19 to be exact—when Sgt. Kennedy walked across the hall to our office.

"Men, I've got some new directives here from Lt. Col. Fraser. I'll put them up on the bulletin board where I want you all to familiarize yourself with them. Don't bother me with any bullshit questions. Just follow the rules and do as you're told." He turned on his heels and walked out.

We sat there, feeling a little woozy from Sgt. Kennedy's out-of-character curtness. Finally, Conroy walked over to the board.

"Jesus Christ will you look at this," Conroy slammed a fist against the wall. "Commencing 1300 hours today, 19 July, all enlisted personnel in Command and Public Information will fully acquaint themselves with the barber shop down the hall.

"Personnel are to pay particular attention to Army Regulations (AR) 614-30, table 7-2 which pertains to the length of hair and sideburns. All mustaches are to be trimmed and should not exceed the length of the upper lip. Boots are to be well polished and cleaned. Pressed fatigues must be worn at all times."

Sitting in the back of the room, Nevin gulped back a nervous laugh. Nobody said a word. Being in Vietnam was shitty enough. Now Fraser was ordering us to act like we were still in the fucking Army.

That night we sat around our hooch, letting off steam about the memo. Everybody except Murphy.

Locked in silence, he took his share of lousy mess hall food, folded it up in his napkin, slipped it into his fatigues' pocket, and took the grub to feed the dogs.

To the rest of us, the dogs were a bunch of dumb mutts. With Colonel Brock gone, they were Murphy's only real source of companionship. There were hundreds, probably thousands, scattered around the base. Growing up in a "civilized society" you forget what it's like in the jungle where everything runs wild. What with Sir Charles roaming the countryside doing what he fucking pleased, no one had the time, energy, or inclination to keep the dog population down, so there were packs of half-starved mutts all over South Vietnam. We were lucky that only three or four of them had taken up permanent residence in the living area outside our hooch.

Mostly we tolerated the mutts. Sometimes we'd feed them scraps from the mess hall or grab a Frisbee and teach them to play catch like we would've with our pets back in the world. Murphy loved them. He fed them. He sheltered them during bad monsoon rains. Damned if he didn't even try to train them.

And, of course, he gave them names—*Kilo*, the biggest one, an off-yellow cross between a cocker spaniel and a German shepherd; *Lifer*, the short, scraggly pug that looked like a drill sergeant; and *Tripod*, the part collie/part everything who'd lost a leg somewhere along the way. Those damn dogs loved Murphy too. Everybody knew it.

Most guys didn't think much about it, because they never saw Murphy "talking" with the dogs. I did. Every night he'd walk the three mutts down to the little footbridge by the 45th Medical Evac Chapel, feed them a midnight snack, show them a few new tricks, and then hold their attention with a slow, pronounced speech.

The more the pressure from Lt. Col. Fraser escalated, the more Murphy sought solace with the dogs. We'd been suffering a daily barrage of bullshit memos. We didn't look right, so he harassed us about our appearance. The paper didn't read right, so he changed the layout. Our hooch area didn't look right, so he harassed us with police calls and inspections, even though he had zip authority in those areas. The fucker was hell-bent on making full-bird colonel. The rest of us be damned.

It was Nevin who figured out that Sgt. Kennedy had been taking some of the heat for us, a fact that became crystal clear during the third week of the Fraser regime when Kennedy abruptly transferred to MACV in Saigon. His replacement was First Sergeant Bobby Lee Baker from South by-God Carolina, whose nose would've been broken if Fraser ever backed up. The two lifers quickly formed a united front, criticizing our looks, job performance, IQ, parentage, patriotism, and the rest.

That was when the graffiti started appearing. It didn't take long to spin out of control, like everything else in this friggin' country. Every day some comment about Fraser appeared magically in the office latrine. One day it was: "Fraser's Emancipation Proclamation— All turds over six inches must be hand lowered by the Lt. Col." Another asked: "How is this toilet paper like Walter Fraser? Tough as nails and can't take shit off nobody."

The best one was: "Lt. Col. Fraser is a thespian." I laughed when I read it and then forgot about it, like everybody else. Little did we know that Sgt. Baker was copying these daily messages and showing them to

Fraser. A few days later, Baker hauled us all into his highness's office.

The Lt. Col. was standing with his back to us, rehearsing his speech when we walked in. He spun around, pissed as all get out. Most days he looked like a ruffed grouse, all puffed up and preening, but today he was a raging bull.

"GIs, atten-hut!" he shouted at us. "Let me get right to the point. Some of you assholes have taken to scribbling slogans about me on the latrine walls. I thought it was funny at first." He paused for effect, and his face moved from scarlet to crimson. "But it's crossed a line and will not be tolerated. Sgt. Baker, will you read the 'messages' from the past few days?"

Baker took a deep breath. "Lt. Col. Fraser is in love with a nig-crow-filly-ache." Everybody in the room started to giggle as we translated the word *necrophiliac* from South Carolinian into English. Baker continued: "Lt. Col. Fraser thinks Vietnamization is a shot you take for gonorrhea."

We burst out laughing. Everybody except Murphy. He just stood there twirling his dog tags and smiling.

Fraser and Baker were righteously pissed off. Fraser was a deep crimson as he told us all, slowly and deliberately: "These slogans represent the ultimate in disrespect to the United States Army. No one is going to leave this office until somebody is man enough to own up to writing this bullshit. NO ONE! It's 1700 hours. We'll stay the whole fucking night if we have to."

I felt like I did in third grade when Freddie Lambert had thrown a spitball at Sister Francesca Regina and we all had to stay after class. We'd still be standing at silent attention in Fraser's office if General McCaffery hadn't come by. Not wanting his commanding officer to think he'd lost control of his troops, Fraser immediately dismissed us.

The battle lines were drawn. On one side of the hall sat Sgt. Baker, Baker's pretty little Vietnamese typist Miss Tran, and Lt. Col. Fraser. On the other side a dozen 71Q20s behind our typewriters, armed with bad attitudes and a fierce determination to thwart the enemy. We pretended not to hear orders. We "misunderstood" everything from A to Z. We developed terminal writer's block. We put typos in Fraser's name and messed up news items he especially wanted to include. If the asshole wanted incompetence, we'd provide it in spades.

The final crisis began on August 19, one month to the day after Fraser's first ass-salt as we came to call his daily posting of Army regulations. We'd thrown a wild DEROS party the night before for Ward who was scheduled to fly out of Tan Son Nhut at 0800 hours the next morning. As we crawled into bed after gallons of beer and bales of reefer, Ward promised, or maybe threatened, to rouse us at the crack of dawn for a farewell drink. I was sure he was kidding.

When Ward actually appeared beside my pillow at five the next morning, I was too wasted to resist, so I obediently crawled out of bed and followed him down to the bar area of our hooch. I didn't expect anyone else would have been stupid enough to answer his call, but goddamned if the whole fucking crew wasn't there—sleepy-eyed, hung over, and mostly dressed in their skivvies. Before I knew it, we were all drinking Bloody Marys—hair of the dog—and toking up. It was like yesterday's party had never ended.

I'm not sure we ever actually said goodbye to Ward, because the next thing we knew, Lt. Col. Fraser's Vietnamese chauffeur, Mr. Trung, arrived with orders to drive us all to the office. It was past 9 a.m. and we were all two hours late for work! Mr. Trung waited outside the hooch while we laughed ourselves silly. Conroy, wearing only his boxers, walked out to the car and gave the driver the word.

"*Dites mon Colonel*," Conroy slobbered in his best high school French, "*que nous ne travaillons pas ce jour.*"

I doubt if Mr. Trung understood a word, but he caught the drift and drove the empty car back to the office.

By early afternoon the dope was starting to wear off, we were out of booze and it was hot as hell, so we decided to wander by the office and cool off in its AC. We dressed, hopped a base shuttle bus, and headed in.

We must have looked a sight. Conroy had shaving cream in his hair, even though all of us were unshaved and wearing yesterday's dirty fatigues. Every one of us needed a haircut. Only Murphy appeared fit for duty, but he wasn't talking much.

The second we staggered into the office, Sgt. Baker ordered us across the hall. Fraser shouted at us to stand tall, but Baker did most of the talking. Speaking in his sweet South Carolinian accent, he informed us that we were a bunch of hippy jerk-off scumbags. His ass chewing was still in high gear when Fraser burst in and escalated the verbal war. He zeroed in on Murphy, shouting into his face.

"Never in my twenty-three years in the military have I met such a sorry bunch of mother-fuckers. You're a disgrace to your uniforms. You're not fit to be called soldiers. You're not fit to be members of Uncle Sam's team. You're not worthy of being wasted by the goddamn gooks! You're a sorry bunch of spoiled, pampered, goldbricking mama's boys. You make me want to puke. I'm going to see to it personally that every last one of you hand-jobs is court-martialed and fined for this morning's insubordination!"

Before the color in Fraser's cheeks had faded, Murphy began to speak quietly. His voice had a poetic rhythm to it, rising and falling as he introduced each point with a punctuated "with all due respect, sir." At first, Baker and Fraser just stood there. We shared their confusion. No one had ever heard Murphy talk this way.

"With all due respect, sir, it was you who embarked on a sustained program of harassment through petty discipline like haircuts and shoe shinings.

"With all due respect, sir, you have never once set foot across the hall to . . . " Murphy's mouth kept moving but we couldn't hear the words because Fraser had grabbed him by his dog tags and was choking him. We could make out a couple more "with all due respect sirs" but we were all stunned by the intensity of Fraser's visible hatred. If he'd directed that venom at Sir Charles, we could have ended the war in a heartbeat.

The longer Murphy kept trying to talk, the madder Fraser got. He shoved his face right into Murphy's and pulled him even harder by the dog tags, accusing him of everything up to, and including, fornication with the base canine population. Murphy simply smiled.

For some reason, Sgt. Baker didn't say a goddamn thing. He knew, like the rest of us, that Murphy had whipped the Lt. Col.'s ass, had spoken the truth about what separated us enlisted men from the brass. As we were leaving Baker's office, he mumbled something almost apologetic about not thanking us for all our hard work.

Before long, Fraser stepped up his counterattack, adding military leaves and R&R plans to his list of targets. He made sure Murphy pulled guard duty every night. Everybody felt like we should do something. None of us had a clue what.

The "Dog Days" memo came down from Fraser on August 24. Nevin pulled it down from the hooch bulletin board and read it in disgust.

"ATTENTION ALL UNITS. From: Lt. Col. Walter Fraser, OIC. To: All IO, PIO and CI personnel. SUBJECT: BARRACKS HYGIENE. It has been brought to my attention that absences due to illness have been interfering with CI and PIO production. Captain Bonner has informed me that this is a result of the diseases being transmitted by the excessive numbers of dogs roaming the base area. Effective immediately, all personnel will commence with the orderly removal of these animals. Be advised that as of 0900 hours on 29 August, dogs not properly tagged and vaccinated are to be shot. Hooches and surrounding areas will be inspected to confirm that this directive has been carried out."

"The slaughter of the innocents," Conroy snorted from the rear of the hooch. Everybody laughed.

Except for Murphy. When I looked his way, he was standing by his cubicle, one hand around his dog tags, the other rubbing his chin.

Later that night, as I walked to the latrine to brush my teeth, I saw Murphy next to the Evac chapel with the dogs. I walked closer, but stopped dead in my tracks when I realized he was giving the dogs some sort of instructions. I eased myself closer to listen.

"Kilo, Lifer, Tripod, sit," Murphy said. The dogs sat. "You guys are going to have to leave the hooch for a few weeks. I know you'll be lonesome and I'll miss you, but it's better this way. Tomorrow I'll walk you over to the bunker line by the bowling alley. You'll stay with my buddy Spec. 5 Davis. I'll come see you every day. But you must stay there. Got that?"

Those goddamn dogs barked right on cue. Murphy kneeled and placed his hands on their backs, like St. Francis blessing the beasts. I shook my head and walked on to the latrine.

Five days later we gathered up all the dogs, loaded them into one of those cattle cars the Army uses to haul GIs, and drove them to the firing range where, every four months, we would take "weapons familiarization," an Army euphemism for target practice. They penned up the dogs and told us to fire our M-16s. I don't think any of us wanted to shoot those lousy dogs. But if we refused, Captain Bonner and his men would and we'd be deeper in the shit. The dogs were going to die anyway, regardless of who pulled the trigger.

I never really liked dogs. As a city kid I hadn't grown up around them much. But that one brief moment gave me a sense of how you could love them. The dogs wagged their tails and barked as if we were their masters. But then they seemed to smell the presence of death. Before we started shooting, they began to throw themselves against the concertina wire, and to wail, a piercing, high-pitched howl that sent shivers up my spine. And then, with nowhere to run, they turned around in circles two or three times and lay down, their eyes crying out for mercy. Then the M-16s took over.

Nevin was right. It really was the slaughter of the fucking innocents.

I can still hear the howling and wailing. I hadn't expected it to be all that bad. After all, they were just dogs. But it got worse and worse as the dogs kept on yelping and whining and crying. Some of them took forever to die. It all seemed to be happening in slow motion, even the tumbling of the M-16 bullets as they pierced the dogs' bodies and burst out their backs. There was blood and fur and dog shit all over the place. And there was a stench of puke from guys who couldn't stomach what they were doing. I did my part.

Murphy wasn't with us the day we shot the dogs. He told Bonner and Fraser he was sick and walked out of the office before they had time to give him a direct order. He wasn't at the hooch or infirmary after we got back. A note pinned to his footlocker from Spec. 5 Davis read: "Murphy, where the fuck are your dogs?"

Two days later Murphy tried to frag Lt. Col. Fraser. He waited for the old man to return to headquarters after lunch at the officer's club. He'd made sure that Mr. Trung wouldn't be in the car. Like a good soldier, Murphy was armed and ready.

The fucking grenade Murphy lobbed in front of Fraser's car didn't explode right away. That gave some sorry-ass private from Amarillo on guard duty time to pull a John Wayne imitation by diving on top of it.

"All you could see after that," Murphy told me from inside his cell at LBJ, "was this poor s.o.b.'s dog tags bursting high into the sky and drifting back down in slow motion. Fuck."

Murphy dropped his eyes. I wondered what he was thinking. That some poor, innocent kid from Texas was killed by "friendly fire" from a crazy-ass private from Minneapolis who was trying to kill his commanding officer?

"I knew that Fraser wouldn't stop unless somebody stopped him," Murphy's voice broke the stillness of the Army stockade. "He isn't an educated man. He doesn't read. He doesn't care. He isn't like us or Colonel Brock. He understands only force. Brute force. The dogs proved it. I knew I had to get rid of him before he hurt somebody bad."

As much as I wanted to feel sorry for Murphy, I wanted to get as far away as I could from him and LBJ and the Army and this goddamn war.

"Jesus Fucking Christ!" Murphy had started weeping. "This fucking place has ruined us all. Every last one of us."

I hear the despair in Murphy's voice every night as I walk past the 45th Evac chapel on my way to the latrine. Last night I noticed three small graves next to the bridge. A carefully lettered inscription reads: "Kilo, Lifer, Tripod: The best dog soldiers the Army ever had."

I do miss Private Dwayne Murphy. And I still miss Colonel Brock. I even miss Sgt. Baker now that he's been transferred up north. But mostly I feel sorry for myself and count down the 96 days I've got left in country under Colonel Fraser's command. That's right. Motherfucker finally made colonel. They promoted him for tackling Murphy after the attack.

To mark the occasion, I scrawled some graffiti on the walls of the latrine.

Brass Tact

Lieutenant Colonel Al Brock sat high atop the cavernous classroom, his senses on full alert. Directly overhead, two large tubes shaped like howitzers spewed recycled academic air, reminiscent of the Tan Son Nhut tarmac on a monsoon Monday. Like a good sentry, Brock observed the shaggy-haired, unkempt students taking their seats in worn wooden chairs with makeshift swing arms that doubled as miniature desktops. Backpacks cluttered their individual LZs. Muted voices delivered coded messages about meetings and Mary Jane and be-ins. Chalkboards stood at attention at 12 o'clock.

Brock glanced down at his copy of Professor Stuart Culver's *Advancing Public Relations* textbook, thumbing through chapters titled "Adjustment and Adaptation" and "Communication and Public Opinion." These were empty titles to him, not strategies he could apply as an officer, a soldier. He caught a glimpse of Culver out of the corner of his eye, giving orders to his teaching assistants and preparing to start the day's lecture.

Next to his textbook was Brock's midterm assignment, a document he was calling "Master of the Strategic Art." Rubbing his shaved head, Brock reassessed his introduction:

U.S. Army Officers are expected to engage in life-long learning and professional development relying on a blend of institutional training and education, operational assignments, and self-development.

"Amen to that," Brock muttered to himself. That's why he was here at the University of Wisconsin in the first place. Culver had convinced him to come to Madison, to take this class, to earn his master's degree, to learn how to influence public opinion. The good professor had even gone out on a limb for Brock, a fellow World War II vet, persuading the UW and the Army War College to add him to the list of more than 100 Army officers Culver would direct in their master's theses.

But Culver hadn't warned him about the UW's daily protests and anti-military fervor. Even out of his uniform, the students in Culver's class knew who Brock was and what he stood for.

In broad terms, Brock's paper went on, *programs and curricula of the War College should be built around the concept of mastering the strategic art, which this paper defines as 'the skillful formulation, coordination, and application of ends (objectives), ways (courses of action), and means (supporting resources) to promote and defend the national interests.'*

Brock wasn't aware he was reading aloud, emphasizing terms like *strategic leader, strategic theorist, and strategic practitioner* . . . Then he uttered aloud his favorite line: *The intent is to focus on how and why one thinks, rather than on what to think.*

"Hey, Pop—can you keep it down over there?" snarled one of the class's more vocal students. Brock didn't know his name but the kid usually dispensed a dirty look in his direction. "Some of us are trying to sleep," he said to supporting laughter.

Brock didn't flinch. *That was it*, he thought to himself, *that's how he would train future leaders, prepare officers, convince the public, and win the war.* Focus on the how and why, not the what. Forget about the kid's comment but instead understand why that's what he's thinking, how these students are caught up in challenging authority, in rebelling.

As a group of TAs fanned out diagonally throughout the large lecture hall, distributing handouts, one of them stopped next to Brock. The hair on his arms stood up. Was the guy targeting him, ID-ing him for the rest of the class?

The TA moved on as the nearby students smirked. The one who called him Pop had thick brown hair that cascaded across his face. The boy's muttonchops reminded Brock of the pet furballs his kids used to put on the doorknobs at home.

Being here was a strategic advantage, Brock realized. Brock would mine that like a mother lode. *...institutional training and education, operational assignments, and self-development.*

Taking in the classroom overflowing with adolescent energy, Brock smiled, knowing that he would become a full-bird colonel, that he would one day teach military strategy at the Army War College, that he'd indulge his grandchildren. He'd write his memoirs.

"All right, let's get down to brass tacks," Culver shouted from the podium, smiling, Brock thought, in his direction. "Please turn to Chapter Seven, 'Defining Public Relations Problems.'"

Raining Frogs in Kuala Lumpur

It was February 2, 1970. I remember the exact day because I was standing in the USARV Information Office's teletype room, arguing with Conroy about which prognosticating groundhog the news services would be covering that day. Being a son of the Midwest, Conroy was making his case for Sun Prairie Jimmy, from Sun Prairie, Wisconsin, "the world headquarters of the groundhog," as Conroy proudly proclaimed.

But as a Pennsylvania native, I held my ground for Punxsutawney Phil.

"Everybody knows who Punxsutawney Phil is," I countered. "He's the reason we even celebrate Ground-hog Day. Hell, they even drive him around in a limo after he makes his prediction."

We kept going back and forth like this, two noncombatants without a clue about what in the hell was really going on with the war and our country. While the three large teletype machines kept banging away at top volume, the war and danger and the Viet Cong lurked somewhere outside, hiding in the bush, waiting for us to get complacent.

I won a case of beer from Conroy that day. He didn't seem to mind. In fact, for grins he placed the story with the dateline "Punxsutawney, PA" at the bottom of that day's *Morning News Roundup*. I can still see him waving a copy of the "rip and read" teletype copy as he roused us from our hard-earned sleep. Raising a carton of milk, Conroy proposed a toast: "Lads," as a huge Beatles and Shakespeare fan, Conroy always called us *lads*, "if rodents can predict the weather in the good ole

USA, then laughter can rain down in Vietnam. Or my name isn't Punxsutawney Phil."

"Rip and read" was indeed the term the old-timers used and that pretty well sums it up. In Vietnam, we updated the old reporter mantra to "rip and release." In both cases journalists relied on the same source, namely teleprinters connected to telephone lines fed by news-gathering companies like United Press International, Reuters, and the Associated Press. We called those revered news sources the Holy Trinity. The three of them were the founts of our Army reporter religion in Vietnam.

The first time I ever set foot, or ear, in the Teletype room at Army Headquarters in Long Binh, I was swallowed up by the endless reams of paper the three machines spewed and submerged in the deafening noise. For a brief moment I was back in college, attending a lecture on the "Model 15 teletype printer." Delivered by a pompous gasbag, the lecture referred to these workhorse printers as "clackers," and now that I'd encountered them, well, I had to admit he was right. The damn things actually did clack, and I mean clack. Standing in the vicinity of three of them—we nicknamed ours Moe, Larry and Curly—you couldn't hear yourself think.

The irony of all this news spewing out into the teletype room in Long Binh, South Vietnam was that it had nothing to do with our jobs as military journalists. We didn't "write the news today, oh boy," or report on what was happening in our midst. Rather, we churned out recurring quantities of puff and propaganda for dissemination through weekly newspapers, quarterly magazines, and scores of homespun news releases about hometown heroes.

So why were the teletypes there in Vietnam in the first place? Good question. At first, we figured the Army brass wanted us to stay up-to-speed on what the traditional media was reporting on Vietnam. Pretty soon, we realized that Moe, Larry and Curley's main job was providing material for one of the Army's more interesting innovations, the *Morning News Roundup*.

The concept was simple. One of us over-educated information types would spend his night at the IO office, babysitting the Three Stooges, finding eight or ten of the more interesting news stories of the day, cutting and pasting them to an 8 1/2 by 11 inch sheet of paper and running them over in two separate batches (one page with 4-5 stories at a time) to the Headquarters' print shop. Lo and behold, by 0600 hours, hundreds of copies of the *Morning News Roundup* appeared at the scores of mess halls scattered across Long Binh post.

The end result was that the homesick troops could have their morning paper with breakfast, just like they were back home in the good old USA.

Some of us were better suited to the *Morning News Roundup* than others. We all had to execute it at some point, but if someone volunteered to make it their regular job, well, that made life easier for guys like me who preferred company and camaraderie. Conroy didn't seem like an obvious candidate. He wasn't your typical Army loner. He just liked doing the *Roundup*.

"I enjoy the quiet, the isolation," Conroy confided to me one night on guard duty. "It's cool being in control." He smiled so broadly that I could see his teeth shine in the deep dark of the bunker. "Especially when you find the one piece that will tickle someone enough to get them to laugh."

After the Groundhog Day story, Conroy decided to always end his two-page (front and back) *Morning News Roundup* with one of these "kickers" as he called them—the quirky, oddball stuff that happens every day in the world and that you could find on the teletypes if you had Conroy's sense of irony. The stuff he found and reprinted in the *Roundup*—like the Vatican's issuing a Ten Commandment-like "Guidelines for the Pastoral Care of the Road" document or a British hotel chain reporting that 95% of the somnambulists in their establishments had been naked men—was so good and so unusual and so funny that mess hall GIs started reading the kicker first so they could at least have smiles on their faces as they were greeted by another fucking day in Vietnam.

That argument on behalf of humor was the one Conroy delivered to the brass when they were threatening to bust him: "Let's be honest," he smiled at his antagonists, "it's not as if there isn't enough doom and gloom in Vietnam, not to mention back home. If one of our primary jobs is to lift the morale of the troops, then that's just what I'm doing."

Whenever Conroy pulled guard duty or was on R&R, one of us had to fill in for him and take a shot at doing the *Roundup*. We didn't even try to compete with him. But Conroy competed with Conroy. The committed communicator had set the *Morning News Roundup* bar so damn high that he couldn't maintain his own standards.

Which was probably how the ersatz Punxsutawney Phil pieces got started.

As Murphy's Law would have it, there came a time when Conroy couldn't find anything that remotely resembled an acceptable—by his standards—kicker. As *Morning News Roundup* press time approached—not wanting to disappoint his faithful readers—Conroy decided to go fictional with the saga of the world's most famous prognosticating rodent.

As offered in evidence by his adversaries, here's how this "rip and release" copy read:

Punxatawney, PA (UPI) - Police were dispatched to Gobbler's Knob today, home of the world-famous Punxatawney Phil, to break up a raucous demonstration. A small but vocal group of out-of-town agitators were protesting Phil's recent prediction of an early spring. Brandishing copies of the Farmers Almanac and waving signs that read "Shadow This" and "Put this where the spring sun shines," the protestors vowed to return. "We will not have our prognostication rights trampled on by an erroneous rodent," said Dick Hertz, the group's leader.

Conroy's second venture into the universe of stories that never made the teletype featured a platoon of counter-demonstrators flocking to Punxatawney and ended with the assembled multitudes chanting, "Phil, our nation turns its frozen eyes to you, boo hoo hoo!"

We all knew what Conroy was doing and that he was bound to take it too far. But what the hell could "too far" mean in Vietnam anyway? Was it Conroy's fault that he wanted to keep guys smiling in a world which didn't offer much in the way of comic relief? It wasn't like he was making up bogus casualty numbers or inflating body counts.

About a week or so after the second fictional Phil piece, Conroy plopped an article about raining frogs in

Kuala Lumpur at the bottom of the *Roundup*. Problem was he did this on one of those days in Vietnam when we didn't kill many and lost hardly any, leaving the brass with time on its hands.

"Find the clown who's writing this shit and bring him to my office," commanded Brigadier General Sullivan.

Before you could say Malaysia, Conroy was in Sullivan's office getting royally chewed out. Best we could figure, the Army's beef with him was that he violated official guidelines for how to keep GIs happy. "Humor unbecoming a military journalist" was probably how they'd put it. Conroy simply cared too much about doing a good job.

When you fucked up at a prime location like Long Binh, you might not get busted, but you'd likely get assigned to the 108th Artillery Group which was the closest Army outpost to the DMZ. They got mortared constantly.

Without Conroy at the helm, the *Morning News Roundup* became just another empty-headed Army assignment. Our hearts weren't in it and we all hated doing it, the quasi-solitary confinement of being alone in the IO office reminding us of the "Twilight Zone" episode starring Earl Holliman when he's walking up and down the streets of a city and can't find a single person to talk to and it starts to drive him crazy. It turns out he's in a space capsule, being tested by NASA to see if he can survive on his own as an astronaut.

That was Vietnam all right. A test without answers. Being stuck in the Twilight Zone.

Eventually, we got word from Conroy at the 108th. *Deeds, not words* was the artillery group's motto, so we suspected he was doing more soldiering than writing. Turned out the Army didn't bust him for the Punxsutawney Phil pieces. Instead they came down on the story about raining frogs. The irony? That one was true. Conroy had the teletype copy in his possession. He shared it with us in his letter:

Kuala Lumpur, Malaysia (Reuters) -- Local citizens were surprised this morning when they awoke to find small green frogs falling from the sky. Weighing just a few ounces each, the frogs landed in trees and plopped into the streets. The Malaysian Meteorological Institute surmised the frogs, native to North Africa, must have been picked up by a strong wind.

Cannon Fodder

While there was an obvious irony in being a soldier named Cannon, the decorated master sergeant would never describe it that way, would never use a term like that. But whatever you called it, the name thing didn't elude his fellow GIs who used it as an excuse to hurl jokes and one-liners in Cannon's direction.

"Sergeant, you are a soldier of very high caliber."

"Knock, knock?"

"Who's there?

"Art?

"Art who?"

"Art Tillery."

Good for them, thought Cannon, going on as they did morning, noon, and night. He laughed along with the guys, because he'd been through two wars and two tours and knew that laughter relieved stress and that soldiers in Vietnam needed all the relief they could get.

Truth was, Cannon needed the release too. The war wasn't going well, and every fresh face that arrived from the States for a 365-day tour was more hostile and less friendly and patriotic.

"No way am I gonna be the last fucking GI killed in Vietnam" was their slogan, and they went about their business as if it was business, and not a cause or a mission. Maybe that's why they were assigned to the Comptroller office at USARV headquarters in the first place. That's where all the business of the war was being waged.

Cannon couldn't relate to this new crop of GIs, which is why the joking around helped. It was like the chaplain said during his sermon last Sunday, "As long as we have laughter, we have hope."

So everyday Cannon played the game, chuckling, pretending to be amused. He wished like hell some of his old Army buddies were there with him, guys like Wilson and Swoboda and Mellen, who understood their role and their responsibility. They'd all gone home and he was on his own, babysitting three dozen goldbricking pencil pushers.

Whatever happened to that war, to those days? There was a lot of laughter then, too, because platoon sergeants with cannon artillery units were usually nicknamed "Smoke." Add that to Cannon's name and it made for an explosive combination. The laughs and the constant wisecracking back then were less personal, more communal.

The chanting of a familiar slogan brought Cannon back to reality. It was a declaration he heard every night, fueled by sarcasm and marijuana.

We the unwilling, led by the unqualified, doing the unnecessary, for the ungrateful.

Nothing funny about that, mused Cannon. Not a damn thing. He knew now that he was done with this war, this Army, and these pacifist pussies. He'd file his paperwork tomorrow and be gone before you could say Ho Chi fucking Minh.

But on his way out, Cannon would have the last laugh. He'd be sure to have the XO pay a house call some night to the IO/Comptroller hooch—the information guys were downstairs but were just as bad as these deadbeats—and get them busted for drug possession.

Some Army, Cannon mused, *when you have to turn in your own guys.*

"Knock Knock . . . "

Battle of the Bulge

The shipments sat inside the rear door of the giant Army Post Office, obscured by mountains of delicately wrapped care packages sent by nervous stateside mothers. Given the popularity of those homemade goodies among the GIs on Long Binh Post, the boxes marked "Cortez" and "Clamato" didn't attract too much attention, which is just the way Myron Swoboda wanted it. The last thing he needed was more grief from his hoochmates about his weight and his love life.

Reason being that the former was out of control and latter was non-existent. The running shoes in the box marked Cortez and the diet beverages, marked Clamato, were designed to help Sergeant First Class Myron Swoboda on both fronts, even in the middle of a war in a far-off land.

His girth notwithstanding, Myron prided himself on being a model soldier. His salute was crisp and tight, his fatigues perfectly starched, and the tips of his jungle boots gleamed in the Southeast Asian sun. Plus, Myron's management of several of Long Binh's larger mess halls, where he oversaw food orders, dining logistics, and dozens of Army and Vietnamese kitchen workers, earned him glowing reviews. Even the mess hall food he served up wasn't bad by Army standards.

"Yo Bodey," some satiated GI would usually yell across a mess. "This shit's almost edible."

Myron tried to play it cool when he heard comments like that, but he lived for those "attaboys," words of encouragement which helped him cope with his daily doses of heartache and heartburn.

SFC Myron Swoboda's heart ached, more than burned, and it ached for Song Le Mai, one of the Vietnamese kitchen helpers at the nearby NCO Club. He loved Mai's smile, her long, jet-black hair, her deep green eyes, and the way she giggled like a high-school girl whenever he spoke to her during a shift at the club.

"Sar-jen Mai Run ver lee fun nee," Mai would laugh when Myron teasingly asked a question. He'd stand there, trying to think of something else to say to her in English, or pidgin Vietnamese, but he'd always get tongue-tied and slink away.

Myron hated that about himself. He knew he needed to stay put, to hold his ground, and open his heart to Mai. Instead he'd open a can of pork and beans or Spam and slurp a couple of Cokes, drowning his sorrows and swallowing his pride.

All that procrastination was going to cease. Signs pointed that way, and Myron was a strong believer in signs, especially when they came in threes. First, there was the note from his old pal Cannon who was working for the Duffy-Mott company in Hamlin, New York, about some new drink called "Clamato" which could lessen your appetite.

Then there was the shipment of running shoes from Bob Bowman, a recent Army retiree from Eugene, Oregon—a fitness nut who'd just joined a jogging program where they wore the special Cortez shoes.

And just the other day, his mother had mailed him three copies of *The Doctor's Quick Weight Loss Diet.* The book jacket described it as "a high protein, low carb, and low fat diet." Myron's mother Millie scribbled a note which said: *Sweetie: Try this on (smile). You should eat six small meals a day instead of three large ones. I lost nearly fifteen pounds the first few weeks and*

am back to a size seven. Here's to seeing less of you!
Love, Mom.

Myron's course was now fixed, his assignment understood. He would lose weight, he would be fit, and then he would retire from Uncle Sam's Army, return home and begin a new life, with his new Vietnamese bride, Sang Le Mai.

But first things first. He, she, and the rest of Myron's rotund recruits were about to embark on a special mission, something never attempted in the Republic of Vietnam. Under his leadership, Myron and his chunky comrades were going to become the "Camp Clamato Weight Loss and Exercise Club."

Pulling it off wasn't going to be easy. It would require as much stealth and skill as any covert military operation. And the undertaking could be risky, too. Myron couldn't bear to think of the ridicule that might be heaped on him if his mission failed.

So, even while the stakes were high and thick, Myron remained undaunted. With all the Army's talk of winning hearts and minds, his "weight loss and exercise club" would reduce Vietnamese behinds and establish his legacy as one of the war's unsung heroes.

And it would win the heart of Sang Le Mai.

As he stood in the NCO club, watching Mai deliver big, juicy hamburgers to hungry and horny GIs, Myron knew he had to move fast. He couldn't bear to watch her slide her delicate fingers into the stack of French fries or sneak a lick of hamburger grease. He knew that as soon as Mai completed her rounds, she and her kitchen comrades would feast on the same high-caloric content. Myron approached Mai's table, operation clearly in mind.

Suddenly, a set of trays crashed to the floor back by the kitchen. Mai jumped, as Sergeant Rob Swenson, the titular manager of the club, rushed over and started screaming at the tiny Vietnamese woman picking up the trays.

"*Du mi ami*," Swenson scolded, leaving little doubt what vulgarity he was hollering at the frightened worker. Myron put his hands over his ears as he looked at the humiliated young woman. Her slim, twig-like figure reminded Myron of Mai's when he'd first met her months ago.

Since then, Mai's figure had changed, now more like a tree trunk than a twig. The larger Mai got, the unhappier Myron became. They couldn't go back to the States this way, like two large shipments of hold baggage.

Myron found himself standing in front of Mai.

"No good," he mumbled, sliding Mai's tray away.

Mai smiled. "GI get his own food. This for Mai." She reached over and stuck her fork in a mountain of fries.

"Too much," Myron slid the tray away from Mai's fork. "Numbah Ten," he added with a scolding face.

"Food good. Mai like," she said, making a counter attack on her French fries.

This went on for several minutes, like a bad Three Stooges skit—Myron sliding the tray away and Mai moving it back. One observer who wasn't amused was club manager Sgt. Rob Swenson.

"Enough of the fucking Chinese checkers," Swenson shouted, smiling a little at his own joke. "Mai, get your ass back in the kitchen." He turned toward Myron. "You Numbah 10 GI," Swenson made a fake scowl. "The bigger my girls get, the better it is for my business."

"*Choi oi*," Myron whistled, trying to keep Mai's attention. "You *dinky dau*. Americans no like fat."

"There it is," Swenson countered, poking a finger in the direction of Myron's belly. Mai giggled her school-girl giggle. "How come Sar-Jen Myron beaucoup fat?" Swenson pulled his eyes sideways as to appear Oriental. Mai kept laughing.

"*Dung Lai.*" Myron shouted, trying to get them both to stop. His face was redder than the ketchup on Mai's tray, so he knew he had to get the hell out of there.

"*Mihn oi!*" Swenson shouted after him with his fake accent, using the Vietnamese word for sweetheart. Mai was still laughing as Myron's heart beat louder and louder with every step he took away from the NCO Club.

Myron headed back to the mess hall to finish taking inventory, but he found himself distracted by his fantasy of making love to Mai, of taking her home and showing her off to his old co-workers at the Piggly Wiggly. Then he thought of Swenson and his heart sank. He would've come down every day on the E-5 if it weren't for the deal he'd just cut with Swenson about the Clamato juice and the exercise shoes.

Their arrangement was pretty straightforward. Myron's materials would be sent to Swenson who'd pick them up with his usual shipments, transport them to the NCO club and keep them hidden, the cans of juice slapped on ice in back of the club's frosty fridge. Myron, in turn, would surrender a cartoon each of Kools and Salems, along with a bottle of Hennessy, to Swenson every Thursday, just before Clamato Club was to convene.

"You should be teaching these dinks how to spread their legs, not slim their thighs," Swenson volunteered during one of their conversations. "A GI needs something to hold on to, not some *baby san* on a diet."

Swenson's grin was as wide as his boonie hat. Myron quickly looked away to avoid Swenson's omnipresent wink.

"You shouldn't talk about them that way," protested Myron. "They're good girls, they work hard, and most of them are working two jobs to support their families. They're not here for your entertainment."

"Sarge, you are living in la-la-land." Swenson rested his long arm on Myron's shoulder. "It's *all* about entertainment. The war, the girls, the clubs, the booze, the dope, the VC—even you and me!"

Swenson dropped his arm from Myron's shoulder. Myron stared at his massive forearm and the tuft of matted hair bleached blonde by the Southeast Asian sun. The sooner he got away from Swenson, the better.

"Lighten up, Sarge." Swenson made a mock salute. "But don't push me too far or I'll tell everybody about your little weight-watchers' scheme."

"All right," Myron shuddered. "You win. See you next week."

Walking back to his hooch, Myron wondered how the Army spawned soldiers like Swenson. This draftee from Minnesota seemed to have his hand in everything that went on at Long Binh Post. Why did the Army allow that to happen?

But this was no time for distractions. Myron had to get his ducks in a row. Over the next few days, he worked on a diagram showing the benefits of Clamato juice and how it was a combination of tomato juice, clam broth, and spices. The Vietnamese liked clams, didn't they?

He drew charts outlining the six steps on the *Quick Loss Diet*. He made a sign that said: "NOTHING ELSE IS PERMITTED ON THIS DIET—NOTHING! IF IT'S NOT

MENTIONED IN THE SIX STEPS, DON'T EAT OR DRINK IT."

When he finished, Myron fumbled frantically through his Vietnamese dictionary, trying to find the right words to communicate his vital message.

When Thursday afternoon finally arrived, Myron summoned the Vietnamese workers to the NCO Club. Women of all shapes and sizes stood in the center of the room, smiling as he entered. One of them pushed Mai toward Myron. The rest giggled. As Mai moved closer, Myron led her to a folding chair and gestured for her to sit down. Giggling, the others copied Mai.

Myron began his presentation, complete with props and charts and gestures. He was earnest and sincere, but his audience doubled over in laughter almost as soon as he started. Adding to Myron's discomfort was the Club itself, which reeked of beer, cigarettes, and hamburger grease. Myron wanted to hold his nose and breathe through his mouth to avoid inhaling anything toxic but that was nearly impossible since he needed his hands free to display his props and brandish his plastic pointer.

By any standard, Myron's Clamato Club meeting was a disaster. To begin with, he didn't have a clue about teaching. Myron rocked back and forth in front of the graffiti-strewn bar, waving his pointer wildly and punctuating the air with his lofty plan. Every portion of his talk took twice as long as he'd planned since Mai, when she wasn't laughing, had to translate everything he said. There was no guarantee that whatever Mai was saying related in any way to what Myron was trying to communicate.

Worse yet, Swenson and his crew repeatedly strutted in and out, using any excuse to parade in front of Myron's class. "Sarge, don't you think the ladies would like to sit on cushions instead of those shitty old chairs? Sarge, can we show your students how to get some real exercise?"

The last straw for Myron was the fact that not one of the women took a single sip from the cans of Clamato juice he'd distributed. Mai in particular turned up her nose. Myron didn't even bother passing around the boxes of exercise shoes.

It was getting late and the women were fidgeting. As recommended by Dr. Maxwell's *Quick Weight Loss Diet*, Myron had begun drinking eight glasses of water a day. He desperately needed to pee.

"Class dismiss..." he started to say when Swenson appeared at his side.

"Take five, Sergeant Swoboda." Swenson patted him on the back. Instead of arguing, Myron hustled to the latrine.

On his way back inside the club, Myron was startled to hear the women singing something that sounded like "Row, Row, Row Your Boat" in rounds. There was laughter, too. At the front of the room, Swenson was conducting the class with a large cucumber as his baton.

When they stopped singing, the women burst into applause. Mai was clapping the loudest.

"Sar-Jen ver lee good swinger," Mai directed at Swenson.

"Honey, you don't know the half of it," Swenson patted her cheek. Myron wanted to run and hide.

"All yours, Sarge." Swenson turned to leave.

"Where you going?" Even to himself, Myron sounded helpless.

"Gotta go. Got *beaucoup* work."

As if on command, all the Vietnamese workers rose to leave with Swenson. Myron pleaded with them, especially Mai, to take their cans of Clamato juice with them. "You drink, Numbah One," his voice rising. "Stay thin, go to America!"

No one turned around.

"Doesn't anyone want to go to America with me?" Myron mumbled under his breath, defeat beating him down yet again. He looked up to see Swenson handing each of the workers two cans of Clamato juice and a pack of Salems.

"You gotta know how the local economy works," Swenson said with a wry smile. "We'll find a way to use the stuff, just wait and see."

* * *

"That's it," Myron admitted to Swenson the next time he dropped by the NCO Club. "This entire damn nation can stay fat and Communist as far as I'm concerned."

"Don't sweat the small stuff, Sarge." Swenson patted him on the back. "These slopes care more about *nuoc mam* than your special brew. Besides, we're just fattening 'em up for the slaughter anyway."

Myron changed the subject. "My buddy in New York said he'll take all the cans back and not charge me for them. Can you return those cases of Clamato juice to the APO today?

Swenson let out a whistle. "No can do, First Sergeant."

"Whaddya mean, no can do?"

"Well, since the slant eyes didn't much want to drink your juice, I did a little experimenting." Swenson waved his hands like a magician. "A splash of vodka, some salt and pepper, a little bit of Worcestershire—a dash of oregano, and voila."

"Volia what?"

"Voila this," Swenson handed a repurposed can to Myron. "The Clamato Cong cocktail."

Myron handed the drink back. "How dare you," he blustered. "You had no right. These cans were for me and my, for me and my…"

"They were for Mai all right," Swenson interrupted. "You wanted to get into her pants and you wanted more room down there to fool around."

Myron was speechless.

"Sarge, after a while you'll realize that the bigger the load the better the ride," Swenson licked his lips. "Lock *and* load."

"Why, you no good, cheating, vulgar . . ." Myron was turning from red to blue to purple.

Swenson squeezed Myron's arm.

"Don't pull that holier than thou shit with me," he snarled. "We're both after the same things—a little nookie and some relief from this fucking hellhole. I'm no goddamn saint, but neither are you."

Myron started to speak, but Swenson cut him off.

"And remember, I know about all your special shipments and your sorry-ass crush on Mai. I have friends in high places."

Painfully aware that all was lost, Myron felt like crying.

"Chins up, Sarge," Swenson beamed. "I can cut you and your buddy in on this action. The wetbacks over at the Motor Pool can't get enough of this Clamato cocktail stuff, so you just keep the cans coming and I'll keep those taco troopers slurping it down. Everybody wins!"

Abruptly, Myron pulled a Myron—he spun around and walked away. Nothing had gone right, but the hell with it. He still had his love for Mai and their future together in America. He'd complete his Army paperwork and drop it off at headquarters the next morning. It helped that Myron was well acquainted with DOD Reg 7000.14-R, Volume 7B, Chapter 1, Initial Entitlement—Retirement. He would fill out the necessary paperwork faster than you could say "Richard Milhous Nixon."

That would get the retirement clock ticking. And that nice little ring he'd bought in Saigon last week—he'd give that to Mai tomorrow, too.

Yes, tomorrow would be better, Myron consoled himself as he turned in that evening. But he hardly slept, awakened by dreams of having sex with Mai in all kinds of public places—the mess hall, the tarmac at Tan Son Nhut, in front of the Statue of Liberty. After he dreamed of making love to Mai on the lawn of his mother's house in Oak Grove, he had to wash the sheets.

* * *

Myron was up before reveille the next morning, completed his mess hall rounds in record time, and marched to company headquarters to deliver his retirement paperwork. He decided to swing by the NCO Club on his way back to his hooch to see just how much Clamato juice Swenson was hoarding. He didn't trust him, and he knew his nemesis wouldn't be here at this early hour, so he could avoid the usual confrontation.

Myron tiptoed behind the kitchen toward the supply room and freezer. There was the long ash of a barely smoked Marlboro in an ashtray on Swenson's desk. His heart stopped.

"Lock and load," Swenson's voice piped up from the supply room. He came out to greet Myron.

"You're up early," Myron stammered, glancing at Swenson's pants.

"Are you admiring my pecker, Sergeant Swoboda?

Myron flinched. Swenson laughed.

"It's all that fucking Clamato juice," Swenson explained. "Man, that shit makes me horny as hell."

Myron remained stoic.

Swenson put his arm around Myron's shoulder, gave it a little press, and started to escort Myron out of his office.

"You try way too hard, Sarge, you know that?" Swenson's voice seemed friendlier. "You don't need to try so fucking hard."

"All I know is trying hard," replied Myron. "That's how I was raised. That's how you survive. You try as hard as you can"

"Just the same, guys like you need guys like me to look out for you, to save you from. . . . "

Just then, there was a low rumble under Swenson's desk. And another. And suddenly there she was, flushed, smiling, her hair tussled, wiping something from the front of her blouse. *Dear god, no!*

Myron stepped back as if he's been knifed through the heart. He could barely stand up, and he couldn't hold back the sobs.

"Mai, how could you? "Myron whimpered.

"Could me wha?"

"How could you deceive me?"

"D.C.?"

"You know, lie to me."

"I no lie, Sar-Jen. I stand," Mai smiled, oblivious to Myron's meltdown.

Myron bolted out the door, the blinding Asian sun hitting him square between the eyes. He stumbled, falling on to a mound of sandbags. SFC Myron Swoboda put his head in his hands and wept, the tears resting on top of a used can of Clamato juice, forming a pool of salt above the big red letters.

Nightly News

The hearty inhabitants of Eveleth, Minnesota, liked to engage in daily pleasantries. The topics of conversation had been the same for years—the weather, hockey, taconite, and kids.

Erik and Agnes Swenson were finding it harder to be pleasant these days. Their son Robbie, like the Lindstrom boy and Herb Long's kid, was stationed in Vietnam. Fortunately for the Swensons, Robbie wrote often and even called home a couple of times.

But that didn't really help them sleep any better.

On October 9, 1969, their TV trays again stood at attention, the beef pot pies sending pockets of steam to the alabaster ceiling, two glasses of milk resting at ease. Five nights a week Erik and Agnes ate dinner in front of the NBC *Nightly News*. They preferred the Huntley-Brinkley duo to the opinionated Walter Cronkite. And they liked that NBC did not play politics with the war, but just gave them informative, daily reports from Vietnam. Somehow, it made them feel connected to Robbie.

Between the commercials for Anacin and Tums, the dour David Brinkley introduced a segment by saying that "a former booking agent for Officers' NCO Clubs in Vietnam, June Collins, testified that club managers had demanded kickbacks. When she complained, she was boycotted and her acts were not hired."

A segment of testimony by June Collins came next. "Sleazy harlot," Erik muttered into his pot pie when he saw the shapely, bouffant-haired Miss Collins. She told her questioners that corruption was widespread in NCO Clubs across Vietnam.

"I don't know of a single custodian who doesn't get kickbacks," she testified to the TV cameras.

"Screw her," Erik shouted at the TV.

Agnes asked nervously, "You don't think this has anything to do with Robbie, do you?"

As if on cue, shots of a U. S. Army base appeared on the TV screen. David Brinkley's voice could be heard in the background: "The potential for graft in Vietnam is enormous. One post alone—Long Binh—has forty-two clubs."

Agnes shrieked. Erik got up to turn off the TV. It took him a while because of his old mining injury.

Before he could reach the set, there were more shots of Long Binh as another reporter, outside a club that looked a lot like Robbie's, began talking. "The more than one hundred such clubs in Vietnam translate into a nine million dollar a year operation," the reporter named Robert Hager stated.

Click.

Agnes was sobbing. "Erik, you don't think?"

Erik looked down on the RCA Victor. His face was bright red.

"I know what I think," he stammered. "I think our son is serving his country and doing his duty. I think we're losing this damn war because of the media and the spoiled college kids." Erik's face turned redder as he added his own private thought. "And I think June Collins is angry because whoever was screwing her, dumped her."

"But what does any of this have to do with the war and what Robbie does?"

Erik sat back down. He and Agnes stared at the blank TV in silence, the setting sun turning the Mesabi Iron Range pink and blue. In the silence, they almost thought they could hear voices saying, "Goodnight, Chet. Goodnight, David."

The Beast in the Jungle

> *Tiger, tiger, burning bright*
> *In the forests of the night,*
> *What immortal hand or eye*
> *Could frame thy fearful symmetry?*
> —William Blake, "The Tiger"

"Can this war get any crazier?" That was the constant refrain from the reporters crowded into the Army's daily press briefings in teeming downtown Saigon. The question always elicited a vocal chorus of "Hell, yes!"

Hunkered down with their colleagues and cigarettes, hands locked and loaded on their gin and tonics, the world's finest correspondents pondered this and other mysteries at "The Shelf," South Vietnam's equivalent of Shanghai's Velvet Lounge and Paris's Ritz. Tucked away inside the old French colonial Continental Palace Hotel, The Shelf provided a roosting spot for every spy, diplomat, profiteer, and Hawaiian-shirted off-duty military type because it was the ultimate source and dispersion point for any news and intelligence worthy of the designation. At the end of a hard day in the streets or out in the field, reporters flocked to The Shelf to exchange information, sniff the air for ripe political and military initiatives, or obtain hints of intended plots and coups. The drinks and the bar girls weren't bad either.

Not only did sages of the war like Halberstam, Sheehan and Browne frequent the place, *Newsweek* and *Time* had their bustling bureaus on the second floor. Visiting VIPs camped out at The Shelf on their way to meet with the generals and ambassadors, double checking what they'd picked up on their official rounds.

It was also a place where hard-edged professional journalists could let off steam, exhaling with a drink, a laugh, and comradely banter. The nightly ritual began with the obligatory "moment of silence"—and a toast—to fallen or missing colleagues. The fact that there were more names on that list every day correlated directly with the increase in The Shelf's alcoholic sales.

"Okay, try to top this." The *Chicago Tribune*'s Dave Van Slyke fired the first volley. The gawky, unpretentious Van Slyke, his tie at half mast, looked more like a chemistry teacher than a war correspondent. "One of our generals, who shall remain nameless—*Abrams*—pulled aside a few of us at MACV today to report that three soldiers from the 54th Signal Battalion had robbed Bank of America's Nha Trang Branch of three hundred thousand dollars in military payment certificates."

There were a few snickers and muted laughs.

"We weren't sure if he was going to deputize us or ask to see our wallets!"

Marvin Jones of the *Kansas City Star* waited for the laughter to subside. He was one of the few remaining veterans of all three wars—Kennedy's, Johnson's and now Nixon's—which gave him near celebrity stature among his peers. His standing was further reinforced by his status as a decorated WWII hero, right down to his military haircut and spit-shined shoes.

"That's easy to top." Marvin's voice bounced off the revolving fans in the bar's high ceiling. "Another of our fearless leaders told me today that Bob Keeshan, otherwise known to most of us as America's beloved Captain Kangaroo, was actually a Marine sharpshooter and that he's supposed to have had something like a hundred and fifty kills in the war."

The assemblage doubled over in hysterics. Someone started singing "smoking cigarettes and watching Captain Kangaroo."

Then it was Harry Carter's turn. New to Vietnam, the baby-faced Carter was still intimidated by his surroundings, afraid of the danger that lurked outside the Continental Palace's walls. As a press corps virgin, Carter hadn't cultivated any sources, so he didn't have much in the way of gossip, stories, or juicy tidbits to share. He'd already drunk too much, lost his ID, and made a clumsy pass at one of The Shelf's beautiful bar girls, but it was his turn, and take it he would.

Weaving as he stood, Carter reached inside his sport coat pocket for the only weapon he had—a copy of a press release he'd been handed a few hours ago by a wiry Vietnamese with a broad smile and a French affect. Trembling, Carter held the single sheet of paper aloft, his hands like pliers gripping a nail. Even as he stumbled over the Vietnamese words in the release, there was no doubt about the message—the Buddhist monks of Xa Loi intended to resume self-immolation immediately unless the United States withdrew support from the corrupt regime of South Vietnam's President Nguyen Van Thieu.

"Party pooper," someone hollered. Carter turned crimson. Quickly, the two old hands, Van Slyke and Jones, came to his rescue.

"Let me see that." Van Slyke walked over and grabbed the release. Jones read over his shoulder.

"How many of you got one of these?" he asked, holding up the sheet of paper. No other hands went up.

"Who put it out?" a voice from the rear asked. Van Slyke glanced at the sheet. "Ah so, 'tis our old friends from the Pagoda." He smiled a big smile.

"You're not going to believe this," he added, handing the release to Jones, "but it specifically mentions quote poet, spiritualist and pacifist Allen Ginsberg as a source of encouragement."

"Allen Ginsberg?" Jones shook his head.

"That fucking fairy," growled a voice near the bar.

"Beatnik."

"Hippie."

"Pansy."

"I saw the best minds of my generation. . . ."

Jones was waving his arms. "Hold it a minute. Nobody knows better than we the truth in the adage about the lessons of history repeating themselves." Low murmurs and rumbling voices.

"What's Allen Ginsberg got to do with history or with Vietnam?" Carter asked.

Jones winked at Van Slyke. He took a deep breath, removed his glasses and raised his hands as if anointing the crowd.

"Once upon a wayward war," Jones intoned in his best Walter Cronkite voice, "Allen Ginsberg graced these friendly confines, stood where we are standing, walked a mile in our shoes, strove with every ounce of fiber in his body to . . ."

"Diddle a Buddhist monk!"

"Enough already," shouted Cutler, one of the old hands from UPI. "My drink's getting warm and I've got a lady friend waiting. Cut to the chase, for fuck sake."

Unperturbed, Jones kept right on talking, "Listen, what we all should know about that time is that it was a lot like this time, which is maybe the way Vietnamese history has always worked."

The Shelf was momentarily shrouded in smoke and silence.

"In the early 1960s, like today," Jones continued, "you had a corrupt South Vietnamese President who was a devout Catholic clamping down on a country that was home to a shitload of Buddhists. The PR professionals will confirm how headlines like 'Buddhist Monk Barbecue in Saigon' weren't the best way to generate support for the U.S. mission in Southeast Asia. And . . . "

Like a practiced vaudevillian, Jones repeated the conjunction.

"And . . .that's when our own Walt Whitman, the intergalactic guru himself, entered stage left. Apparently Ginsberg thought he could lower everyone's temperature by his mere presence. Ooohhhmmmm ..." Jones started chanting.

"Well, did he?" Carter asked.

"Truth is, our home-grown cosmonaut spent most of his brief time here scared—and I use the world in its literal sense—shitless."

A volley of laughter moved like a wave through The Shelf. Most of the reporters stopped talking and looking at their watches to listen to Jones.

"Tell them what Do-Re-Mi said about Ginsberg," Van Slyke reminded him.

"Good point," Jones smiled. "Even the fresh faces among us know Do-Re-Mi, real name Ngo Rai Minh. He was at the center of the Buddhist uprising in '63 and was famous for his impromptu press conferences about the Buddhist burnings.

"Legend has it that when Sheehan asked Do-Re-Mi what he thought of Ginsberg, the cherubic bonze replied matter-of-factly: 'He's a spy.'"

A wave of laughter rippled across The Shelf and out into Tu Do Street.

"But not just any goddamn spy," Jones shouted above the laughter, "he claimed Ginsberg was a quote top secret, CIA-clearance spy!"

More hoots and shouts.

"So, Ginsberg spends a couple hours chanting 'Om' with the monks who basically ignore him. After the combat police flattened the Pagoda gates, it suddenly dawns on the cosmic cowboy that this is a pretty dangerous place, so he spent the rest of his time here hiding in Sheehan's office."

"'I'm scairt,' he wrote to his boyfriend back home." More snickers. "And within four days, the poet laureate of pop was long gone. Probably had to pick up some clean underwear."

Jones paused.

"You all know what happened next. More Buddhists toasted themselves for the benefit of the six o'clock news. Diem and his brother dug their hole deeper and deeper until Kennedy and the CIA had no choice but to take them out. And the rest, as they say in Vietnam, is mystery."

Jones made a royal bow, applause raining down from his colleagues.

Hours later, the applause echoing in his ears, Carter lay awake in his bed, a delicate flower of Southeast Asian femininity breathing quietly next to him. Sleepless, he remembered seeing the 1963 protests on the six o'clock news back home in Richmond. His thoughts drifted to his days at the university, the all-hours debates with his dorm mates about God, religion and fate.

His first marijuana high, and his romantic lows. And Allen Ginsberg and his favorite lines from "Howl":

> yacketayakking screaming vomiting whispering facts
> and memories and anecdotes and eyeball kicks
> and shocks of hospitals and jails and wars,

Which sent him on to a restless sleep.

Morning came early, the sun bright and boiling, the monsoon preparing its regular noon appearance. Jones and Van Slyke joined Carter for the stroll to 89 Huyen Thanh Quan Street. The Xa Loi pagoda, separated from the street by a gated fence, shimmered like a jewel in an otherwise drab downtown. Inside the fence, they were welcomed by a stone Buddha holding a vial of elixir in one hand and making a gesture that seemed to signify the removal of obstacles with the other.

"Left hand know what the right hand is doing?" pondered Van Slyke. "Could be a metaphor for the U.S. in Vietnam?"

The interior courtyard resembled a travelling carnival with scores of monks, nuns and children zigzagging the premises. Amid the cacophony of bells and chants arose a stench, a rotting, cabbage-like smell which brought the three reporters' hands to their noses.

A wrinkled *mama-san* in black pants flashed her stained teeth and beckoned for them to follow. She guided them to stairs which led to the main hall of the pagoda on the upper level, then stopped, pointing to the stairs on the left hand side and saying something in Vietnamese.

"What's she jabbering about?" Carter asked the others.

Neither of the men said anything. The *mama-san* kept pointing. Jones finally spoke up.

"She wants us to take the stairs on the left," he said, "because that's how men enter the hall. Females enter on the right."

As the trio ascended the stairs, Jones started to hum his favorite Glenn Miller song, "Let's Build a Stairway to the Stars."

They entered a huge, pillar-supported rectangular hall. Looming above them was a massive statue of Buddha, seated in meditation on a lotus blossom, wearing the garb of a monk.

"Pleased to meet you," Carter mumbled in his best Mick Jagger accent, "hope you guessed my name."

Jewelry hung from the Buddha's ears. He had closely cropped curly hair, and a large protuberance on his head. Carter knew from his "Introduction to Religions of the World" class in college that these indicated something, but he forgot exactly what. Royalty? Aptitude?

"I don't think we're properly dressed for the occasion," whispered Van Slyke.

Do-Re-Mi's smiling face appeared. He bowed and escorted them down the rectangular hall. With his plain robe and shaved head he looked like a miniature version of the statue.

At the back of the large hall, seated in a circle, were the Pagoda's elders in flowing robes that reminded

Carter of Gandalf in *Lord of the Rings*. Their sleeveless tunics, trimmed with yellow brocade and yellow silk, made them appear like tiny starbursts.

One by one the monks, with Do-Re-Mi translating, spoke about life and death, Buddha and Vietnam.

"The struggle of the Vietnamese people is not only for peace and independence," came the translation of the words of the first elder. "The struggle of the Vietnamese people is to remain Vietnamese."

When Jones tried to ask a follow-up question, Do-Re-Mi held up his hand. Another bonze spoke. "A dog is not considered a good dog because he is a good barker. A man is not considered a good man because he is a good talker."

That was the way it went.

"An idea that is developed and put into action is more important than an idea that exists only as an idea."

"A jug fills drop by drop."

"My editor's going to love this," snarled Jones, imagining the ball-busting McMillan cursing him out for delivering a scoop consisting of windy epithets. What was the monks' strategy? What were their demands? When were they going to take action?

As if the Buddhists sensed his thoughts, the oldest monk spoke, in quiet tones.

"All of life is sacred," he began, speaking in near-perfect English, "but life has to be lived."

The monk paused.

"Look at us. We are the walking dead. We are mere puppets. Our beliefs, our traditions, our way of life—are all dying. But even death is not to be feared by one who has lived wisely," he smiled.

He and the others stood, bowed and left the hall.

Van Slyke put his hand on Jones's shoulder, trying to keep him from exploding. Carter looked pleadingly at Do-Re-Mi, who had a twinkle in his eye.

"One more question, yes?" He smiled at the trio. Van Slyke and Jones were reaching into their pockets to withdraw their reporter's notebook when Carter blurted out, "What does burning human flesh smell like?"

Do-Re-Mi stood and smiled.

"You'll know it when you smell it," Jones grimaced. "It stays with you forever."

The tiny monk nodded.

"I had to write about it in 1963 but it really described itself." His voice sounded more like a coroner's than a reporter's. "Burning skin melts and, well, it smells like charcoal, but not any charcoal I've smelled before, or since.

"When a human body burns, the iron in the blood gives off a coppery, metallic odor," Jones was growing pale. "And the body's internal organs smell like burnt liver. But," he glanced at Do-Re-Mi, "the monks say when one of them burns, it smells like musky, sweet perfume."

Do-Re-Mi smiled and nodded.

"Mistah Jones understand because he's been there. He first to write about Thich Quang Duc, the 73-year-old monk, who first burn himself in June 1963.

"You come today," Do-Re-Mi was looking directly at Carter, "and you see how monk burn, outside to inside, layer-by-layer."

"Dehydration, ignition," Jones was muttering. "The heat dries the skin; the dry skin ignites. That fire, in turn, dries the next layer of muscle and fat, which then ignites. And so on, until the internal organs are consumed. Textbook."

"Vietnamese Buddhist give off, how you say, 'modest BTUs,'" Do-Re-Mi smiled. He turned and began to walk toward the statue of Buddha. "Three o'clock outside Ba Huyen Thanh Quan."

The three reporters walked back to the Continental Palace in silence. The heat was draining. Soon, the monsoon would follow. And then the immolation.

"Jesus, it's today," Carter burst out. Jones and Van Slyke looked at him. "This is June 11th, the anniversary of Thich Quang Duc's suicide!"

"Give the Cub Scout journalist his history merit badge," Van Slyke said, turning back to the business at hand.

No reporters showed up to cover the 3 p.m. performance. It didn't matter. They could smell it, nauseating and sweet, putrid and steaky, like leather being tanned over a flame. The smell was so rich that you felt full. They found out later that the smell and the taste had a name, Do-Re-Mi.

The next morning each of the journalists went his separate way—Carter to Pleiku, Jones to the Delta and Van Slyke to Nha Trang. They never saw one another again.

Several years later, Carter received a copy of "Verses Written for Student Antidraft Registration Rally" by Allen Ginsberg. Two phrases were highlighted in yellow.

"*The warrior is afraid . . .*"

"*The warrior has a big trembling heart.*"

Scrawled on the back of the envelope, Jones had written: "You never really lose the smell of burning flesh. No matter how long you live."

Looking out at the Beirut landscape, hands trembling, Carter pulled the blinds, sat down on the edge of his bed and wept.

Fearful Symmetry

Nightfall in the jungle was like living in another country. The dark overwhelmed and enveloped so that everything and everyone succumbed to it. No latitude and longitude. No battle lines. No Catholic and Buddhist. No black pajamas.

Just the dark.

Nightfall was also the time when the jungle came alive. You'd hear the constant drip, drip, drop of water falling from trees, the ribit ribit of throaty frogs, even the occasional scratching of small ground animals foraging for food. And other sounds that defied United States Army classification.

All this disquiet helped keep you awake on watch— but it would play tricks with your mind. You'd start to tell yourself that when you didn't hear the jungle's natural sounds, that's precisely when you'd be in deep do-do.

One some nights, *this* night, the quiet was too much to bear. You could even hear it, and you wanted the silence to stop. You wanted to stand up or scream or jump or run. Or even just reach down to scratch your balls or remove a leech.

Then every fiber in your body froze. There was that noise, the one from before, the one you couldn't pinpoint. The mounting monsoon rain intensified the noise. There it was again—and again. Some kind of a low, guttural growl—could that be possible? And movement; yes, definitely some movement.

Suddenly, the source of the growl made a sudden leap.

MOTHERFUCKING GOD IN HEAVEN!

Pandemonium and sheer terror. Screams. A huge cat had pounced out of the darkness, seizing something or someone in its jaws.

A TIGER!

Someone fired a flare, and in the fleeting yellow light you could see what looked like a tiger's paw pinning a soldier to the ground. Shots. More screams. Another flare Why the fuck didn't you fire? Would it come for you next? Piss ran down your pant leg.

And then the darkness returned.

One of the grizzled veteran reporters from Reuters Wire Service would tell you later that "Tigers kill very quickly, usually by ripping the spinal cord at the neck with a blow from their front paws," he'd make a snapping gesture with his hands, "or by biting through the skull," he'd smile a malevolent smile and grit his teeth. "They would never try to eat something before they killed it first."

By the Time I get to Phoenix...

I entered Saigon's Imperial Bar. I didn't even finish asking my question when the bartender pointed me in the direction of Phuong Thao. The place was crowded for a weekday afternoon, mostly military brass and Five O'clock Follies reporters. It was blue with cigarette smoke and a haze of strong perfume. I heard the strains of a sappy Carpenters' song playing in the background. The bar itself was decorated in full tropical décor, as if any of us needed to be reminded where in the hell we were.

My guide was the Imperial Bar's maître d', Lucky. His alabaster face seemed to collapse around some wrinkles in the middle and his smile reminded me of Peter Lorre in "Casablanca." For a minute, the entire scene reminded me of "Casablanca," down to the parrots staring at me and tracking my movements from their bright yellow cages behind the bar.

"She beau-te-fulll girl, Phuong." Lucky ran his tongue over his lips in my direction. "You maybe like bang bang with Phuong?" He leered his Peter Lorre leer. "You know her Vietnamese name has special meaning. Phuong veerly special," Lucky whistled.

He pushed me in Phuong's direction, but I resisted. I didn't want to appear too eager, or too cowardly. Stealthily, I slid toward her, observing how perfectly the slits of her turquoise *ao dai* hung proportionally over the sides of the bar stool. She wore black trousers beneath the *ao dai*. I stopped behind her to admire the colorful birds pictured on the back of the smooth, silk garment.

Phuong smelled like chrysanthemums, and, for a moment, I felt like I was walking on one.

"'Scuze you, GI," Phuong snapped in my direction, following immediately with her Imperial Bar smile. I was tongue-tied, and as awkward as if I were back at the 8th grade dance at Most Blessed Sacrament. Phuong could be the most beautiful woman I had ever seen.

"Hey, it's okay. You buy for me Saigon tea." Phuong got immediately down to business. All I could do was stare.

"What American GI always say 'Kaz got your tongue,'" Phuong laughed, lifting her *ao dai* so that I caught a glimpse of the beautiful white skin between the slits and her trousers.

"This here Spec. 4 Bailey," Lucky gestured toward me. "He write for Army paper and *Stars & Stripes*. He write story about Imperial Bar so we get more bizness," Lucky smiled a big smile. "He want to intervue beau-te-full Saigon g'rl who visit Imperial Bar to make GI feel better about being far away from home. You be nice to him and tell him good story."

Lucky headed off to negotiate short-term contracts for his other star players. Phuong waited for me to say something.

"Thank you for doing this," I finally spoke up. "It won't take long."

"Lucky pay me, so I okay," Phuong volunteered. "You still buy for me Saigon tea?"

I tried to get the bartender's attention. Phuong turned her chair, her knee brushing against my leg. Had it been this long since I'd been with a woman, sat next to a woman, tried to talk to a woman?

Wanted a woman. This woman.

I looked at Phuong's face. It was so bright, so radiant, that I instinctively reached for my sunglasses. That impulse reminded me of Murphy. Damn! I came here for him, not for me.

"I bring greetings from a very good friend, His name's Murphy."

Phuong just stared. Not even a flick of the eyebrow.

"Dwayne Murphy," I continued. "Big GI, very funny, red hair, long sideburns." I gestured with my hand to my own sideburns. "Always wears sunglasses." I held mine up to her. "Talk very very fast. He talk about you."

Phuong cast her eyes around the bar. I looked for a damn bartender. I knew I'd lost her. I played my trump card.

"He told me he calls you 'Foxy Phoenix.'"

Phuong's face burst into a warm and knowing smile. Like a nervous suitor, I kept talking.

"Murphy says you are very special. He says your name has to do with the bird phoenix and is one of four Vietnamese girls' names that represent the four sacred mythical creatures. You special girl."

"Me like Murphy. He make me laugh." She paused and her face grew dark. "But he in trouble."

"How did you know that?"

"Ly tell me, she Lucky's sister."

"How does Ly know?"

"Her boyfriend Bao work at Long Binh. He say Murphy kill GI."

How in fucking hell did these people know everything that's going on?

Lucky reappeared, this time with an officer on one arm and an older Vietnamese woman on the other.

"You ask Phuong about Bar, not about bad t'ings," Lucky then made a sweeping gesture toward Phuong.

"Major, may I present Miss Phuong Thao for your dining pleasure."

I reached for Phuong's hand but missed and my arm brushed her colorful *ao dai*. She looked back at me. Nothing.

"What are the other three?" I asked, almost inaudibly. Phuong gave me a puzzled look. "The sacred creatures? Murphy asked me to ask you."

Lucky grabbed Phuong and began to escort her and the major off to a table in the dining room. The parrots screeched in Vietnamese as the bartender placed a Saigon tea on the bar in front of me.

A Lean, Well-Painted Face

It was late in the war and nearly everyone had left Saigon except a one-time temptress who sat in the window of a building where a bar used to be. Day and night the traffic passed by, and the woman liked to sit late because it helped her remember the old days. She would sit and stare out the window for hours upon hours. Two janitors would watch her because they didn't want to work and they were attracted to her ancient beauty.

It was monsoon season, late in the Year of the Pig, and the janitors sat together at a table close against the wall near the door of the building. A steady stream of soldiers went by in the street. The janitors made fun of the soldiers who were too young to understand their dialect.

The woman knew what they were saying and she hated them for it. She hated the soldiers, too. She hated all the Americans who had abandoned her in this shattered place. She harbored a special hatred for the young men who fell in love with her, boys really, whose eyes were dreamy, whose lips were dewy, and whose souls were empty.

The janitors would tease her about having lovers who committed suicide.

"Who would kill himself for you?" they'd ask her. "Didn't they know you would grow old? That they would have to leave?"

She thought of the tall red-haired boy, the one who swore to the moon and the sky that he would never leave.

"She stays up because she likes it," said the older janitor.

"She's lonely. I'm lonely. You're lonely. We're all lonely." The younger janitor spoke riddles to the Saigon night.

The woman looked over at them.

"You do not understand," she told them. "This was a clean and pleasant bar, well lit."

Neither of the janitors knew what to say.

"Good night," the younger janitor, sounding defeated, stood up to return to his work.

"Good night," the other said.

The woman sat and stared out the window at nothing. The janitor turned off the flickering light. She continued her own conversation. She recited a Buddhist prayer from her childhood, one she used to repeat when her lovers would beg, weep, or shout.

"May all sentient beings have the courage to look within themselves and see the good and bad that exists in all of us," she spoke to the darkness. "May we open our hearts, shining the light of love into the dark recesses where doubt and fear reside. May we have the courage to step into that light and embrace whatever we find, letting it rise to the surface freed by the act of loving kindness. . . . "

She thought of her past, remembering the light, which had always been good.

Herded Through the Grapevine

I hated pulling guard duty for a lot of reasons, but I hated it most because it reminded me that I was in the Army—and in Vietnam. Something about putting on a helmet, carrying that goddamn M-16 and a bag of ammo magazines, filling my canteen, and marching out to the bunker line as if I really was a soldier—man, that was an Aqua Velva wake-up call.

Every time I put my hands on that sleek, black barrel, it would trigger a nausea that enveloped my entire body so that every inch of me felt like it was about to puke. I never admitted it to anyone, even though I was relatively safe in the air-conditioned jungle at Long Binh.

When I wasn't on guard duty, I tried hard to forget I was even in Vietnam. During the day I'd pretend to be working on a real newspaper, not the piece of crap Army propaganda rag I helped edit. Even while I was pounding out some bullshit about winning the hearts and minds of the Vietnamese peasants, I envisioned myself in the role of an ace reporter for a hard-charging publisher like Charles Foster Kane, pushing to uncover the next big scoop.

I spent my down time in the IO hooch watching reruns of *Bonanza* and *Room 222*, or sitting outside watching movies. In either instance, high.

When that got old, I'd listen to rock and roll albums or tapes, hanging loose in the purple haze, avoiding all the other war shit.

Except for guard duty. That was real Army stuff. You couldn't bullshit your way through guard duty because it was too real. Nobody can lie and B.S. for that long without slipping up. Nobody stuck over here anyway.

The only compensation was that if you were lucky, you could spend eight hours of your life in the dark with somebody cool or interesting. Like Jackson. Before that night, which is why I'm telling you this, I'd suffered through a couple disastrous bunker mates. One was a Jesus freak from Missouri who spent all night trying to convert me. "Go and make disciples of all nations, Matthew 28:19," he chanted. "Go where you wanna go, do what you wanna do," I shot back. "John Phillips 1965." That pissed him off no end.

The other douche bag was this kid from Hawaii who cried a lot about how shitty he was treated by all the other racial groups in 'Nam and back in Hawaii, not that I had a clue what that meant or why I should care. I figured the "Kauai Kid" had dropped some bad acid.

Given my track record, I wasn't looking forward to wasting another slice of my life with some redneck, pussy, or Holy Roller, but I definitely lucked out with Jackson. He had some really good shit, so we smoked and settled in, listened to a little music, sang a few bars, and set about debating the pros and cons of the 'Nam grapevine.

But first we had to endure the customary Army rigmarole before we ever got to our bunker, including the usual back-and-forth between the field officer of the day and us flunkies.

"What are the general orders?" The man of the hour was a shake and bake type fresh out of Officers Candidate School. Like hung-over altar boys unsure of our liturgical Latin, we muttered back something about "guard everything within the limits of my post" and "quit my post only when properly relieved," then grabbed our dicks to illustrate our interpretation of the sacred text.

After Jackson and I got our buzz on—judging by the taste he'd laced his joints with a little opium—he started painting these dazzling verbal pictures, word-portraits of Vietnam that somehow sharpened my sense of where we were and what our being there had to do with the grand scheme of things.

"Imagine, *mon ami*, that we are seated in a lush and fragrant French rubber plantation," Jackson intoned, using an accent that made him sound like Pepe Le Pew. "Tres bien, non? Long Binh is ze bright shining star, and each point of ze star is connected by channels of water—what we Francais call 'trenches'—to a series of star bunkers."

"Where are you, little star?" Jackson's voice jump cut from Paris to Philly as he suddenly burst into song. "*Whoah-oh-oh-woh-oh,   ratta-ta-tata,   too-oo-ooo.*" Jesus if he didn't sound just like one of the Elegants.

Fucking Jackson went on like that all night—presenting Long Binh post as a many-pointed French star, visualizing Greek gods hewing rocks to construct the steel-reinforced concrete bunkers, even scaring me a little when he described the trenches snaking around the base with such a hiss in his voice that I swore there was a viper in the bunker.

"There it is!" Jackson shouted, prompting me to jump about three feet off the ground. "The bunker is a great place to hide, but not such a great place from which to fight!"

Followed by a lively rendition of "Nowhere to Run, Nowhere to Hide."

Maybe it was the dope, but I could see every detail of everything Jackson's voice conjured up. I didn't have to tell him; I didn't need to talk really. I just sat there and enjoyed the command performance.

Our only difference of opinion had to do with the Vietnam grapevine, the local source of gossip and opinion that drove everybody crazy. For some reason, as soon as Jackson brought it up, I launched into a rant about how you couldn't trust the 'vine but you couldn't avoid it either.

"Fucking thing is a grab bag of fiction, fact, disinformation, gossip, and propaganda," I argued, pointing out that grapevine sources included officers, enlisted men, private contractors, Vietnamese workers, prostitutes, correspondents, and no doubt a few VC. I was cataloguing my grapevine grievances when Jackson put up his hand, signaling for me to pause.

"Relax, brother," he exhaled in my direction. "The grapevine frustrates everybody, which is what makes it acceptable. The real quandary is whose version of 'I Heard it Through the Grapevine' is better—Marvin Gaye's or Gladys Knight and the Pips."

We both broke down laughing, until we eventually realized the commander of the guard was on the radio, checking in with the guard post. Jackson hated answering to anyone's orders, so I was ready to sign on for our bunker.

When the commander called on Bunker 763—us— Jackson responded by improvising the lyrics of a then-popular Paul McCartney chart topper, opining about how U. S. Ambassador to Vietnam Ellsworth Bunker might not approve of how we were waging the war. By the time Jackson was repeating the chorus, you couldn't hear the commander of the guard screaming at us over the voices from the other bunkers singing along. A couple of flares went off along the perimeter line and, for a moment, we became that fantastic French star Jackson had described earlier.

By the time the MPs got to our bunker, Jackson and I were doing a kick-ass version of the Flamingos' "I Only Have Eyes for You," inserting a lyrically-appropriate critique of American foreign policy.

The Army brass was royally pissed and assigned us all extra guard duty. Jackson got slapped with an Article 15. A few nights later, he pulled his stunt at the Bien Hoa Theater during the showing of *Woodstock*, and they hauled his ass to LBJ.

Today's grapevine carried the news. Jackson had offed himself.

"That boy waz just some hippy-dippy doper strung out on somethin'," Top explained to us as we prepared for guard duty. "That sorry SOB probably pissed off everybody at LBJ, so he had no choice but to hang hisself."

Whatever did go down, it hadn't stopped most everybody on post—lifers and draftees, old and young, black, brown, yellow or white, whether they knew Jackson or not—from forming their own opinions about what went down and why. That's how the grapevine worked—it allowed you—reader or listener—to make your own story, turn the page and carry on, not having to spend too much time wondering why some disaffected GI would allegedly commit suicide without telling anybody why.

Top was one of the good old boys, and he didn't know what he didn't know, which was also one of the grapevine's tenets. What the grapevine couldn't communicate to lifers was why a '60s generation draftee like Jackson wasn't just some Dr. Spock-coddled goofball who got high and spoke out because he had a problem with authority.

No, Jackson was a genuine hippie ambassador for those of us who'd surrendered to Vietnam and the draft rather than go to jail or Canada. The dude was a bright light, one of the few who reached high and never looked back.

So, what do I think? Fuck the Grapevine. Fuck Top and the Army. Fuck LBJ and the Viet Cong. Fuck Woodstock, too. I promised Jackson's memory I'd get to the bottom of this. I'd act like a real goddman journalist for once instead of the sanitized Army propagandist I'd become. I'd do my job, get people to talk, dig out the truth, if there was truth anywhere in 'Nam.

And I'd remind them that it was the Smokey & the Miracles' version of "I Heard it Through the Grapevine" that we eventually decided was the best. Fools didn't know that.

Rest in peace, brother.

The Revolution Isn't Being Televised

None of us knew much about him except that his last name was Jackson and he always wore sunglasses. Even at night. Somebody said it was because he was high all the time and his pupils were dilated. Nobody knew for sure.

Jackson would just show up at our office out of nowhere. He'd hang out and work on his company's newsletter. What he was really good at was getting us high on the kick-ass dope he smoked. Most days we were fucked up on the job, it was Jackson's doing.

He was also our main source for what was happening stateside. Reading *Stars and Stripes* and the sanitized versions of *Time* and *Newsweek* left us clueless about what was really going on, so we depended on Jackson's insights.

The night before the shit went down, he'd told us how happy he was with the way things were going back home. America was owning up to its responsibilities. Before 'Nam he'd been everywhere from San Francisco to the Big Apple, he'd hitchhiked from upper Michigan to Key West, Florida. Everywhere he was struck by the same good vibes—people were getting high and flashing the peace sign.

He'd talked a couple of us into going with him to check out *Woodstock* at the Bien Hoa base theater. Before the movie, we went out to the bunker line with some other REMFs and got wasted.

"Brothers, was Woodstock the greatest thing that ever happened to America or what?" Jackson asked rhetorically. "How's the movement going here?"

"Shitty," someone volunteered.

"It'll get better," he smiled. "You've got everything here at Long Binh—discontent, quadraphonic sound systems, lots of soul brothers, and great dope. Things will go well here."

None of us said anything.

Jackson pretended to be our drill sergeant and marched us to the theater. We sang cadence about Jody and our girlfriends, adding a couple choruses from "Coming into Los Angeles."

Later at the theater, they stopped the film just as Sly and the Family Stone were cranking up the volume on "Higher." The lights came on, and a voice told us that the VC were nearing the perimeter and we had to get to a bunker. With the movie's sound track off, we could hear mortars exploding and sirens sounding. Most of us started moving dutifully toward the exits.

Jackson refused to leave. He was standing on his seat, arms raised, singing at the top of his lungs.

"Feelin's gettin' stronger... " he yelled at the screen. Sly shouted back, telling Jackson he was going to take him higher and higher. The rest of us had already left the theater.

The last we saw of Jackson he was wearing his shades and giving the peace sign as the MPs led him away. None of us did anything to help him.

Alice Doesn't Live Here Anymore

We all had rituals in Vietnam. The brothers had their dap, the grunts had their boonie hats and bracelets, the zoomies had their high-class clubs, the lifers had their Vietnamese lovers.

What we had late in the war, way back in the rear, was TV. Not the TV that brought the turmoil of the world into your living room on the six o'clock news. No, for us it was the kind of TV that reminded us of growing up, of sharing rites of passage with families like the ones on *Ozzie and Harriet*, *My Three Sons,* and *Leave it to Beaver*. Bummer about the Beaver, buying his lunch in Vietnam. Kinda made sense though, when you think about it.

For the hard-charging, hard-working, gung-ho REMFs in the USARV Headquarters' Information Office, the TV ritual was watching *Room 222* which had premiered on ABC around the time most of us were initiating our acquaintance with the Army and Vietnam. It reminded me of the 1967 movie "To Sir, With Love" with Sidney Poitier playing an idealistic teacher dealing with rambunctious white high school students from the London slums. The TV version was based in L.A., but the lead character, Pete Dixon, was black and cool, just like Sidney Poitier.

Watching *Room 222* every week was the one thing that brought everybody in the hooch together. Juicers liked it, dopers liked it, loners liked it, our resident lifers liked it—hell, even our one and only soul brother liked it.

We did more than just watch *Room 222*. We would *live* it, or at least pretended to be living it for the 30 minutes it was on. Nevin or Conroy would warm things up by making a bold prediction about who would be the focus of that episode's story line. Then they'd make things more interesting by establishing odds and laying bets.

It was the night after Kenny Martin's visit. I can still see Nevin walking up and down the hooch with a clipboard and a sheet of paper, puffing on a Lucky Strike and wearing a green visor on his head like Uncle Billy, the bank teller in "It's a Wonderful Life."

"Fifteen minutes, boys and girls," he shouted through puffs of smoke. "Just fifteen more minutes to place your bets."

"Who will it be?" he continued in his carnival barking manner. "Our favorite history teacher Pete Dixon? Walt Whitman High School's long suffering principal Seymour Kaufman? Liz McIntrye? Or how about everybody's wet dream, Alice Johnson?"

Shouts of "Alice, dear sweet Alice, I love you Alice, I want to screw your brains out Alice" rained down on Nevin, a shared vision of Karen Valentine, the cute young actress who played student teacher Alice Johnson on the show. Something about her perky smile, her luscious lips, her mini skirt and high socks. Hell, everything about Alice Johnson had the entire hooch moaning with pleasure.

"Or will there be a dark horse tonight?" Nevin continued. "Helen Loomis? Wild-hair Bernie? Or how about our favorite militant Jason Allen? Or resident genius Richie Lane?"

By the time the show started, Nevin had collected an assortment of cigarettes, ration cards, Military Payment

Certificates, and joints, all of it, in theory anyway, to be paid out to the winners. He posted tonight's odds on the blackboard that hung next to the refrigerator: 2-1 in favor of Alice with Principal Kaufman second at 5-1. A surprising Richie Lane held third place at 10-1 while regulars Pete and Liz were out of the running.

Alice always got the most votes because, well, we all desperately wanted every show to be about her. However, the rhythm of the series that we'd been able to detect pointed to the brooding principal as tonight's likely focus. That usually translated into something heavy or meaningful like race or pregnancy or bigotry which meant less of Alice. Damn!

Before we got completely settled in, Conroy warned everybody about making too much noise. "It's okay to shout when Alice appears, or when Pete comes on," he intoned, waving his can of PBR to the multitudes. "But keep it down during the show so we all can follow what the hell's happening. We'll have the usual post-game discussion immediately after the broadcast."

Sometimes the best part of watching *Room 222*, besides the camaraderie, was talking about it afterwards. Like the night we dissected how and why Principal Kaufman burned out and quit, arguing for hours why he should or shouldn't go back to work. Or the episode about the freshman girl with a crush on Pete who tagged along on his dates with his girlfriend Liz.

And, of course, any show about Alice.

So far the episode that had provoked the most intense all-night debate (fueled by beaucoup beer and reefer) was the one where Walt Whitman High started its own radio station—call letters KWWH of course—compliments of an egotistical city councilman who arranged to have the station built at the school. Eventually, the pompous ass went ballistic because the Walt Whitman students start to broadcast programs criticizing school board policies. Might have seen that one coming.

That episode hit home for us because it seemed so much like the Vietnam we knew and the AFVN radio we listened to morning, noon, and night. By the end of our back-and-forth, we had arrived at a consensus that the Walt Whitman kids had more balls than we did. At least they'd gone after the guys in charge. Mostly we rolled over and played dead.

Tonight, Conroy sat down to cheers as the show's inane theme song filled the Vietnam night air. Full of anticipation, we glued our eyes to the TV. An unlikely bunch of 20-somethings, thousands of miles from home in the middle of a jungle and a fucked-up war, we sat watching a TV show more or less about ourselves. The fictitious Walt Whitman High School in *Room 222* is our high school, the place we want to be tonight, every Wednesday night. Now light years away.

That night's episode was entitled "If It's Not Here Where Is It?" and you could tell within the first few minutes it wasn't up to *Room 222* standards. Not even Alice could save the situation. That night our favorite show was a little too topical, a little too close to home.

The subject was Vietnam.

Guys started to hoot and howl at the entrance of the alleged 19-year-old "Vietnam veteran" returning to Walt Whitman to resume his education. The guy was a gold-plated cliché. He didn't fit in with the other students, couldn't handle authority. The whole fuckin' nine yards. Even stalwarts like Pete Dixon and Seymour Kaufman spouted sanctimonious bullshit. And Alice, sweet Alice, never showed.

Eventually, Ward walked over to the TV and turned it off. Nobody said a word.

"Now hear this," Nevin jumped up and contorted his face like James Cagney in the movie "Mr. Roberts." "Now hear this. All contributions to tonight's war widows and pensioners retirement fund will be immediately returned to their rightful owners."

He was trying hard to lift our spirits. A few of the guys started to smile. "It has come to our attention that the commanding officers of *Room 222* have gone AWOL and been replaced by hard-charging lifers in need of a promotion," Nevin pointed his finger in the direction of USARV headquarters. "We regret any inconvenience this may have caused. I repeat, all contributions will be returned."

Nevin handed back the wagering materials as most of the guys cleared out. A few of us lingered, feeling let down, deceived.

"They didn't have to remind us we were in Vietnam," Ward was pointing at the TV. "That's just not fucking   fair."

The Medium is the Message

"Who the fuck watches TV in Vietnam?" Kenny Martin asked me that question the one night he spent in our hooch. He was on his way back up north after some in-country R&R. He'd just come off several rough weeks in the field, and he didn't want to talk about it. He didn't even want to get high.

So we drank a few beers and reminisced about college, about coeds, and mostly about the days we'd spent together washing dishes in the women's dining hall. Even though Kenny and I later became fraternity brothers, it was those first few weeks together as freshmen, shaking our heads at the mountains of discarded food and trying like hell to differentiate Dawn Smith from Jackie Mills, seeing their midriffs as they came through the line that had forged a bond between us.

Now here we were, doing our post-graduate work in Vietnam. One a grunt and the other a REMF. Still struggling to figure out who was who.

There was so much that separated Kenny and me and our Vietnam experiences that we couldn't even begin to talk about it, which is probably why we focused on the past. But reminiscing couldn't make us forget where we were. Or where we were going. I was headed back to my job in the air-conditioned jungle in the morning while Kenny had to return to the real jungle. He wrote me later to say he'd asked for reassignment when he got back to his unit but was turned down. He wanted to be a REMF, he admitted, and it was all on account of the night we were together. It wasn't on account of anything I said. It was what Kenny heard.

As I blathered on about our college days, Kenny's grunt ears perked up at the sound of something unusual. It was the din of our hooch TV blaring in the background. That now became our topic of conversation.

"You guys really have a TV?" he asked as if he'd just discovered gold. "And it works?" I nodded affirmatively and Kenny shook his head as if stunned to discover electricity in Vietnam.

"What do you *watch*?" he asked almost in a whisper.

I didn't want Kenny thinking we had all the comforts of home, so I tried downplaying the TV.

"We only see what the military brass wants us to see," I lied. "None of it is any good."

Kenny wasn't buying it.

"So you get news and sports and, like, real shows?" Kenny's eyes were big as saucers.

"The news is censored, the games ended a week ago and the shows, well, it's mostly old crap like *Bonanza* and *Combat.*"

At the mention of *Bonanza*, the face of the young Kenny from college reemerged. He was somewhere else, with the galloping horses of the show's theme song, watching the flames burn the map of the Cartwright spread.

"Wow," his whole body spoke. "What I wouldn't give to see an episode of *Bonanza.*"

But *Bonanza* wasn't on the AFVN schedule in Saigon that night, so Kenny missed getting reacquainted with Hoss and Little Joe. A week later when Kenny rejoined his unit in the bush, he got to see a terrific program called *NVA Night Attack.* I missed that one.

The Gospel According to Shortimer Sam

Shortimer Sam was so damn short he needed help just getting his socks off the bottom shelf. He'd DEROS in 11 days which meant he'd been in this hellhole for 354!

The place just won't be the same without him. That's because Sam was the U. S. Army's ambassador of astute advice. He was our Ann Landers, Dear Abby, and Billy Graham rolled into one.

I had my own selfish reason for not wanting Sam to return to the World, mostly on account of the brass wanting me to take over his column. No way I could be Sam. The guy flat out knew how to give advice, knew when to be tough and when to be kind. Not to mention he could cite every stinking Army rule and regulation verbatim.

Like the letter last week from some PFC in the 229th Aviation Battalion.

Dear Sam:
Can you tell me if the 229th Avn Bn has been award-ed the MUC? If they have, am I eligible to wear it even if I wasn't here when they got it?
- PFC ALG, 229th

To which Sam replied:

Dear PFC:
The 11th Avn Grp received the Meritorious Unit Ci-tation in GO 3006, dated 20 June 67. It was for action Sep 65 to Nov 66. The 229th Avn Bn was added on

the first order, in GO 787, dated 21 Feb 68. If you served for 30 days in the unit during the cited period, you wear the MUC as a permanent decoration.
If not, you go bare.
- Sam

Fucking A, only Sam could know that.

He could be funny, too. Like the question he got a couple weeks ago from a GI named "River Rat."

Dear Sam:
Me and some of the other guys think we saw a submarine on the Vam Co Dong River on patrol the other day. We hadn't been in the sun that long so it couldn't be heatstroke. It didn't look very big but it operated under the water and came up every once in a while.
What's up? Or should I say, down?
- River Rat

Dear Rat:
I did a little reconnaissance myself and here's "What's up, Doc."
There is indeed a thing that operates in the Vam Co Dong. In fact, what you saw was a 50-gallon water drum operated by an ex-VC Navy Captain who thinks he's Burt Lancaster. He has a crew of three on board with him and they float around looking for Clark Gable.
Run Silent, Run Deep, GI.
- Sam

I'd proved my point. Life in Vietnam would be a lot worse if it weren't for Sam's weekly comments and insights. I just wished he'd have taken me under his wing and let me watch him work because he'll be gone soon and I'll be shit out of luck. He may have written a lot, but he sure didn't talk much.

When Sam was preparing his last column, he stopped by my hooch and asked me to meet him out on the bunker. For some reason, when Sam had something on his mind and felt like communicating, that's where he liked to talk.

It was late. I was sitting around in my skivvies and sure as hell didn't feel like doing anything. But, it's Shortimer Sam, so I grabbed my official green Army t-shirt, put on a pair of cutoff fatigues, strapped on my Ho Chi Minh sandals, and headed outside. It was hot as hell.

I found him sitting on top of the green nylon sand-bags that covered our bunker.

"Read this." Sam shoved several sheets of paper in my face and handed me his Government Issue flashlight with MX-99I/U marked in big letters on the side.

"What the fuck, Sam," I sputtered, trying to hold the flashlight and the pages in my hands.

"Please don't swear," Sam requested.

"Okay, but what do you want me to do with this?"

"Read it over a couple times and give me your reactions." Sam talked like his columns read. "I value your opinion."

"Read it? I can hardly see it."

"Here, I'll hold the flashlight."

I could see Sam staring at me in the humid darkness. His most distinguishing feature, his unibrow, looked like the ribbon on a typewriter.

"Sam, if you really value my opinion, then you'll let me take this back to the hooch and read it there."

"I can't let you do that," he shot back.

"What're you talking about?"

"Someone will see it, and if they know you've read the rules, then Shortimer Sam won't be meaningful."

"Come again?" I wasn't accustomed to someone referring to himself in the third person, as if he were some kind of objective observer. And give me a fucking break on what was, and wasn't, meaningful in Vietnam anyway.

I decided to tell Sam just how fucking ridiculous he was acting when he yanked the flashlight away. It flickered under his chin, throwing a ghostly light on the rest of his face. That look reminded me of Bogey's face in the scene from "The Treasure of the Sierra Madre" when he started going crazy.

All of a sudden, I was spooked.

Frightened or not, I made up my mind to get the hell out of there. But when I tried to stand, my cutoffs stuck to the sandbag and my shorts rode up my crack. Sam wasn't

speaking, but I detected a faint sound in the jungle night, one that came from the direction of the Officer's Club. The tune seemed familiar enough but the singer's voice was a mix of Don Ho, Eric Burden and Charlie Chan.

"Jesus, those Filipino bands sure can ruin any song," I laughed. "Who knows? Maybe they're playing that Animals' song for shortimers like you." I turned back toward Sam.

He was gone.

* * *

Later on, I was back in my hooch, sitting on the edge of my bunk. Night had finally descended upon Vietnam and all my hoochmates were asleep. I grabbed a towel and toothbrush and stumbled down to the latrine. I brushed my teeth slowly, replaying my conversation with Sam. Did I misunderstand him? Offend him? Miss some signal that I was supposed to pick up? Or did I just imagine the whole thing?

Back by my bunk, I knelt down like I did every night to pray to whoever was out there watching over me. I noticed a large brown box, almost the size of my foot-locker, stuffed under my bunk. There was an envelope with my name on top of it. I tore it open.

"Dear Soon-to-be Shortimer Sam:

Your time is at hand 'cause I'm outta here.

And that's how it goes—no goodbyes, no hand-offs, no "this is my last column" b.s. Our soldiers need to believe that Shortimer Sam is constantly here for them, always listening and advising. Never DEROS-ing!

You'll find everything you ever wanted to know about Army regs and protocols and procedures in this box. Apply it at your own risk. But realize that what passes for communication is nothing but acronyms, abbreviations, titles and shorthand.

Trust your instincts, your <u>human</u> instincts, not your Vietnam-invented ones. You know the rights and the lefts. You know where the bodies are buried, and you know who's holding all the cards.

So, keep your head up, GI, not down, and remember these reporter's rules of editorial engagement:

1. If a soldier complains about feeling bad, he either has malaria, the trots, VD, or all three.
2. Answers always raise more questions.

3. Never drink Agent Orange for breakfast.
4. Gonorrhea is just a four-letter word.
5. Ribbons are for typewriters, not uniforms.
6. When Army lifers shake their heads to tell you no, listen for all the noise inside.
7. Recess is what GIs want more than anything.
8. You have no idea what a quagmire is.
9. You'll get at least one letter every week signed by The Beaver.
10. Words can pile up like dead VC—save a life, drop an adjective!

Yours is the most important job in the Army because you give our troops truth, hope and humor. All the Shortimer Sams who have gone before you expect you to regard that old Smith Corona typewriter in the USARV IO office as your keyboard, your umbilical cord, and your elixir. Now, give it everything you've got!
-Sam IV

So, this is what Sam had handed me tonight? It sure seemed un-Sam like. How did he come by the wit and the wisdom? How could he be so consistently accurate, in-charge, mocking, and entertaining all at once? How in the hell would I do that?

Rummaging through the box, I uncovered some answers. For one, it was organized a helluva lot better than the Base library. There were categories for everything from awards to citations and medals, from discharges to R&R and hold baggage. And the fucking replies were there, too, already crafted, with just that right touch of Shortimer Sam irreverence and humor.

There was more. Endless sheets of paper with scribbling in ink and pencil, letters and notes signed by guys calling themselves "Ed the Head," "Tokers for Truth," and "GIs for Justice." There were also plenty of copies of an anti-war GI newspaper that we'd only heard stories about.

The more I dug down into the box, the more letters I discovered. Ones that asked questions like: "Why is it that the little man gets all the shitwork and hassles while the higher-ups get their asses kissed and tickets punched?"

Even more notes and letters that sang the praises of pot and getting high. None of these ever saw the light of day, or a response from any Shortimer Sam.

As if that wasn't enough, cartons of expertly wrapped Pall Mall packs of marijuana cigarettes sat at the bottom of the box. The note on top read:

> *Sam:*
> *You'll be flying high in the friendly skies. Trust us—a joint a day will keep the blues away.*
> *Peace & Love,*
> *The Central "High"land High Rollers*

I opened a pack and admired the tightly manicured marijuana joints. I walked outside and lit up.

Does it make any fucking difference? I asked myself, *if I write what's real or simply repeat the party line?* Everybody, myself included, knew what was going on by now, and I doubted if they'd believe anything that was written in a goddamn Army newspaper.

I shook my head. It wasn't just the marijuana talking. I fetched Sam's box and hauled it back outside. In less than three minutes, I figured somebody was going to be in my face, asking me what in the hell I'm doing. But that was still three minutes away.

I flipped my butane lighter, grabbed a stack of Shortimer Sam-addressed letters and set them ablaze. I tossed them back inside the box and watched that catch fire, too.

The smoke rose ever so slowly, making lazy little clouds. *Words are made up of letters that are really symbols which are supposed to carry meaning,* I told myself. But the letters that make up the words don't stand for shit, really.

All we've really got, I determined, *is our own experiences and interpretations.* Mine were still forming. Sam's were over.

Watching the smoke trying to climb into the humid Vietnamese night struck me as a metaphor, and I laughed because that's the kind of thing I'd just denounced by setting the box on fire. I listened for the sound of the Long Binh fire truck but instead picked up the strains of "We Gotta Get Outta This Place," either in my head or out there in the great Southeast Asian silence.

Delta Lady

"Take a hit off this." Specialist Four Charles handed me one of his tightly manicured marijuana cigarettes. I had no idea where he got these, but Charles always had a pack of joints on him, cellophane and all. It was by far the strongest dope I'd ever smoked.

We crept our way along the shortcut to our office, through brambles and brush and sometimes sandy terrain, passing the joint. It wasn't a long walk, and it was partly illuminated by lights from basketball and tennis courts. Every time I took this route to USARV headquarters, day or night, I tried to envision this place as the rubber plantation it once was. The Michelin tire guy was about the best I could come up with.

Before you knew it, we'd arrived at the big, bright sprawling "H." Ours was the north building of the H, the two-storied metal one that looked out over most of Long Binh. There were more people out there than in my hometown. Most nights, we would sneak back into our office, put on our headphones, turn on our reel-to-reel tape decks and listen to music as we typed letters home to our wives and sweethearts and family.

Nights like those when we took that trek we were so goddamn high it was as if we weren't even in Vietnam. Those few special minutes transported us elsewhere—back to college or away on R&R—any fucking where but Vietnam. Sometimes, that sense of being someplace else lasted long into the night, since the music and the typing kept us aloft even as the dope wore off.

And some nights the dope never wore off.

"Procuring marijuana in Vietnam is easier than getting a beer at a keg party," I remembered the JAG officer telling us during our in-country orientation. He looked like one of the Beach Boys—shiny blonde hair, toothy smile, square jaw, perfect features. I kept waiting for him to burst out in surfer tunes.

"In every camp in country," he lectured to a roomful of us newbies, "a GI can get a joint within five minutes."

I was seated near the front, so I started taking notes.

"The weed grows wild. It is cultivated by the Vietnamese, who rarely use it themselves," he went on. "They understand marijuana's proclivity as a new cash crop."

Even though I wasn't exactly sure what proclivity meant—it sounded kind of dirty—I burst into a grin. Hell, this was the best lecture ever, since we were finding out all we needed to know about the weed we already knew and loved.

Now the Beach Boy major pulled down a map of Vietnam with big Roman numerals on it and armed himself with a pointer. "With three harvests a year, the Mekong Delta is the marijuana bowl of Vietnam." He thrust the tip of the pointer on IV Corps. "Recently, police moved in to destroy these crops because many of the local farmers were giving up rice and turning to cannabis."

Momentary frowns.

"But the destruction urged—and supported—by the Army and United States federal agents hardly touches the supply."

I looked around. All the guys were smiling the big shit-faced grins that can mean only one thing.

And then I was back at the typewriter, high as a fucking kite, writing to my old lady back home, complaining about how terribly awful Vietnam was and how I couldn't wait to get back home. The music had stopped.

Blue Ribbon

Before he was drafted, Stevie Potter was studying to be an Ag Extension agent. He wanted to follow in the muddy boot prints of his father and grandfather and help every Iowa farmer grow bigger and better crops.

Stevie was always more at home in a field or a barn. He excelled in FFA and 4-H and usually won the soybean competition at the Chickasaw County Fair.

Stevie lived for the feel of soil in his hands, the smell of dirt, the texture, the minerals, the possibility. The farm was his classroom, and he was passionate about spreading the gospel of growing things.

Maybe that's why, as the Army ramped up its pacification efforts in Southeast Asia, they sent Stevie into the villages first. The Vietnamese farmers welcomed him, and Stevie'd learned enough about growing lowland rice that he'd join them in the rice paddies during the harvest. That was a strange sight, Stevie, built like a fireplug and not much taller than the scrawny Vietnamese, using a knife to harvest the rice. He'd top that off by accompanying the farmers as they walked their water buffalo over the rice to take out its grain.

It wasn't Iowa, but as long as he was in Vietnam, Specialist Four Stevie Potter was the unofficial expert on Vietnamese farming and the Army's chief authority for telling the difference between farmers and guerillas.

"Look here," he'd tell his fellow grunts, holding up his buddy Morgan's hand. "All you need to do is look at their hands. Soldiers aren't like farmers. They have one callus, right here, on the trigger finger," he pointed to Morgan's finger. "See?

"Farmers, they've got hands just like me," Stevie continued. "Fucking calluses everywhere."

Stevie Potter and his farmer hands no longer work the fields of Vietnam. He, and they, are in Long Binh Jail. Stevie lost it the day the company headed south and the M113 tracks cut through some rice paddies. When the Vietnamese farmer got pissed and started hitting the lead track with his rake, the Troop Commander got out to calm him down and the old guy hit him, too.

Next thing you knew, the tracks were going sideways instead of single file, destroying everything this old peasant lived for since way before Uncle Sam ever got there. The long file of American ingenuity, sporting nicknames like *Fortunate Son, Easy Rider, Babysan, Spooky*, and *Boonie Rat*, steamrolled side by side through the old peasant's fields.

Little Stevie Potter walked up to the TC, pulled out a M1911A1 .45 automatic pistol and pointed it in his face. Stevie's callused, farm boy's hands caught on the trigger and the gun kept shooting, the TC's brains joining the other seeds in the soil's rice seedbeds, awaiting the next harvest.

The Art of War

Most nights I lie awake, imagining I'm hiding in a bunker. It's pitch dark and so fucking quiet that I can hear the heat.

Without warning, sparks fly, weapons erupt, and waves of Viet Cong attack my position. I shit my pants as they come full speed, AK-47s blasting, bayonets yearning for my flesh. My hands freeze, and I can't pull the trigger. I hear voices shouting, cursing, begging me to shoot.

"Pussy! Coward! Traitor!" they scream. But I recoil. Torrents of blood breach the bunker. It runs hot and smells of iron and copper. It's above my head, and I'm choking until I finally roll out of the bunker somehow. It's so dark that I can't see my body, but I reach down with my right hand and discover my leg is gone. My other hand is shattered in pieces, and my senses are overcome by the scent of my own blood, at first sweet and then fouler, rotten.

My flesh is ripped by AK-47 rounds and punctured by bayonets. I'm falling, tumbling, crying, pissing, moaning—seeing the face of the colonel's driver or the post barber looking down on me, a knife in his mouth, a black headband on top of his head. He's smiling malevolently as he begins to slice my ears and then my eyes and. . . .

"You still writin' that shit?" Edwards asked. I jump, and then pretend I'm adjusting my BVDs so he doesn't think he's startled me.

"Yes, sergeant, I'm still writing this . . . ." I respond matter-of-factly.

"Son, when are you gonna put down that pen and join this man's Army?" Edwards loved playing this game with me, but I wasn't rising to the bait. We both knew what he was really interested in was learning why I write in the first place.

"Didn't you hear me, boy?" he bellowed like a drill sergeant. "Time's a wastin' and you best get your college-educated head out of your ass."

I sighed. Edwards and I were the same age, the same build, the same background—hell, we were damn near the same person, except that while I matriculated at Kenyon College, he was washing cars, getting married, joining the Army and doing tours in Germany and I Corps. Vietnam, more than the lives we lived in the USA, had finally brought us together.

"Can we not play this game just now?" There was a slight begging in my voice which surprised and disappointed me. "I've told you a hundred times before—I write because it helps me to deal with this shit, to get by. It's like my therapy." I paused. "It's like you frequenting the whores at Cholon." I made my pretend Chinaman face. "Same same."

"Can I help it if the slopes find me irresistible?" Edwards said turning his back and twisting his arms around his neck, making it look as if someone was lustily embracing him. Fucking guy had to be double-jointed. I had to admit it was one of his funnier moves.

"What they find attractive is your MPC." I held out some Army script in his direction. "If you're out of money, you don't get no honey." I pulled the bill back from his hands.

"Okay, let me get this straight." Edwards sat down on the edge of my bunk. "I fight the enemy, put my ass on the line, and sign my life away to Uncle Sam while you smoke dope, read books, and write in your journals. So, you're the model soldier and I'm the fuck up?"

That was so good I had to write it down. I figured Edwards would be pissed if I quoted him verbatim, so I waited until our hooch maid Bau Mau walked by because I knew he'd forget about me and start flirting with her. I needed to get his words down when I could because Edwards was the only guy in our office of college grads and would-be journalists who'd actually seen any combat. In my stories, I changed his name to Sergeant Cannon because I thought it was a funny pun.

As I watched him teasing Bau Mau, I kept thinking that we were both acting our parts—me the innocent, wet-behind-the-ears college boy and Edwards the grizzled, uneducated combat soldier. He was Aldo Ray and John Wayne; I was Montgomery Clift and James Dean.

"Just what are you doing, Specialist?" His inflection triggered a change in our exchange. For the moment, Edwards had resumed his role as the higher ranking NCO.

I didn't answer.

"Spec. 5 Bailey, I asked you a question."

"Yes, Sergeant Edwards, I heard your question," I replied in a soldierly fashion. "And I do not have an answer. Sir." I added the "sir" to piss him off. It worked.

"Look at these stripes, Specialist," he pointed to his sergeant's insignia. "I work for a goddamn living, son. Don't ever call me sir!" He was smiling again.

"And if you're going to write down something about me," he winked, "make sure to start with how Vietnamese women find me irresistible."

Edwards got up from my bunk and started to walk out of my cubicle. He stopped abruptly, wound his arms back around his neck and shoulders, and started cooing in a pretend Vietnamese woman's voice. "Ooh, sar jen Edwarz, you veery veery big and strong . . .oooh, sar jen . . ."

As Edwards exited the hooch, I wrote down his earlier comments: *"I fight the enemy, put my ass on the line, and sign my life away to Uncle Sam while you smoke dope, read books, and write in your journals. So, you're the model soldier and I'm the fuck up?"*

* * *

I was telling Edwards the truth about my writing, sort of. The war was so astoundingly cruel and surreal that I relied on writing to center me, if that was even possible in Vietnam. Otherwise, I'd be constantly reminded of what a shit show this place was. Over time, I'd grow numb like everybody else, eventually not batting an eye when we took *Chieu Hois* out for one-way chopper rides, fudged on the numbers of KIAs, or didn't say squat about the fragging epidemic at Long Binh and all over fucking Vietnam. Shit, if we couldn't find and kill the Viet Cong, we'd kill ourselves.

Yeah, I needed my writing more than it needed me. At times, I'd just sit back and take it all in, seeing things as if I were some character in a Fellini movie. I mentioned that to my buddy Ward when we were having a beer at the 90th Replacement Battalion last week, and kept seeing this same GI walk by with a live snake coiled around his neck.

"Jesus, will you look at that," I nudged Ward when snake man passed us for about the hundredth time. "That shit is right out of a Fellini movie."

Ward had no idea what I was talking about.

"I've never seen a movie about cats," the flat-footed E-4 from Buffalo, New York replied, "but that fucking snake is scary."

The writer in me mined film analogies for all they were worth. Mainly because they were true. Not a day in Vietnam went by when you didn't hear somebody talk about a GI "pulling a John Wayne" or "pretending to be Audie Murphy." For sure we all knew we were smack dab in the middle of the ultimate Vincent Price horror movie.

Adding an even more bizarre aspect to this was the fact that a lot of nights we'd blow a number, grab our lawn chairs (yes, lawn chairs in Vietnam) and head over to watch an outdoor movie. We'd sit out in the Southeast Asian night, scores of America's finest, drunk and stoned, watching *MASH, I Never Sang for My Father, The Baby Maker, Easy Rider* and whatever other celluloid the brass had decided might help build morale. When the credits rolled and the lights came up, it was like getting a two-by-four upside your head—you're not at a drive-in back home trying to unhook Nancy's bra, numbskull; you're in fucking Vietnam with umpteen days to go.

I had two all-time favorite movie nights—*King Kong* and *The Green Berets*. The *King Kong* thing started as a joke between me and Ward, and then snowballed to the point where we forced everybody in our area to go— even bribing hoochmates like Richards and Mancini who never went anywhere. We put up signs all over the place with pictures of Uncle Sam and King Cong—we changed the K to a C—that read: *"We Want You!—at tonight's movie."* Underneath in small letters we added *"Dance afterwards."*

We got totally smoked up and filled nearly half the outdoor pavilion. We cheered like crazy every time Kong appeared and booed the airplanes as they buzzed him on the Empire State Building. Everybody else thought we were crazy.

The Green Berets night was even more intense. That's because while most of the audience were draftees or young enlistees like us, a good number of lifers showed up to watch John Wayne. Reminiscent of a high school mixer, we claimed one side of the pavilion; they camped out on the other. Their lawn chairs sat in perfectly straight lines and rows; ours resembled a Chinese fire drill. They were drunk; we were stoned. They cheered for Duke and the Green Berets; we jeered him and laughed at them, all of them.

Toward the end of the movie, as the sun was setting in classic Hollywood Western fashion, John Wayne's character patted the head of the little Vietnamese kid and said, "You're what this is all about." Ward jumped up as if he'd been shot out of a cannon and shouted at the screen.

"You goddamn idiots; the sun don't set over the South China Sea!"

One of the lifers threw a bottle that barely missed Ward's head. Somebody tossed a chair at the lifers. The projection weenies stopped the movie right away. There was a lot of pushing and shoving and name-calling, but we were all too wasted to kick the shit out of one another.

Nights like that I imagined the VC spying on us, preparing to attack. *If I were them*, I thought, *I'd blow us away right there and then.* Shit, not even John Wayne could have held off the Indians with a fucking lawn chair.

* * *

Writing made Vietnam a book and not a movie. Vietnam was surrealistic, apocalyptic and euthanistic rolled into one, and words were the only way I could even begin to handle it. The war could be terrifying on paper, but it was an ugliness I could control since I was the one writing it down. I'd write it and read it without having to live it. I didn't have to kill anyone.

What this meant was . . . well, I'm not quite sure what it meant. I know it distanced me from the lunacy and enabled me to change points of view, altering names and dates and places, inventing dialog, even scripting happy endings where they didn't exist.

Edwards was the only one who ever paid any attention to what I was doing. Most of the other guys were college grads, 71Q20s like me, so they were always writing a lot, in and out of the office. Edwards was the exception. He wasn't a 71Q20, information specialist; he was the USARV Command Information office's very own supply clerk. Which was weird because none of the other hot shit USARV offices had one assigned to them.

Supply clerk wasn't his MOS either, but Edwards didn't seem to care. He'd enlisted right out of high school for some military job he never got. Faster than you could say "Ho Chi Minh," the SOB was in 'Nam, knee-deep in some pretty bad shit, got shot up and shipped statewide with a couple of medals. He spent a little time at Dix as a drill sergeant, did a brief hitch at Kaiserslautern, got divorced, then back to Vietnam, specifically our red, white and blue newspaper office and our little slice of the air-conditioned jungle.

* * *

Watching over us from his desk in the back of the office, Edwards was part Greek chorus, part Big Brother. Even though he was our chronological peer, he seemed older, sitting back there like an exam proctor with his cap on, his big dark rimmed glasses reminding me of Doctor T. J. Eckleburg in *The Great Gatsby.* A trio of us English majors in the hooch had this on-going argument about F. Scott Fitzgerald's good doctor, debating whether he represented God staring down upon and judging our society as a moral wasteland, or a symbol of the essential meaninglessness of the world.

Shit, all we would have had to do was open our own eyes to see how meaningless our fucking existence was. But we didn't. Edwards did, or at least he appeared to, from his perch in the back of the room. Of course, he didn't have a clue who Gatsby or Fitzgerald or Eckleburg were. But his eyes were always on us.

As far as we could tell, Edwards didn't do much work back there. He drank Coca Cola, smoked cigarettes, and flirted with our cute little Vietnamese receptionist. He was an expert at catching flies out of thin air. He'd snag them, throw them to the ground, killing them instantly. There was a huge fucking pile of them on the floor under his desk.

Every couple of weeks, Edwards would broadcast from the back of the room that we had better get our supply orders into him "pronto," one of his favorite words, if we wanted any pica paper, glue, rulers, paper clips, autographed posters of Raquel Welch, or whatever. He always ended his broadcasts with some stupid ass joke none of us thought was funny.

"Papasan say 'man who lose key to Tran's apartment get no new key.'" Give me a fucking break.

When we stood down back at the hooch, we rarely saw Edwards. He never smoked dope with us, never watched TV, never participated in the nightly Botticelli contests where we showed off the real benefit of our college educations—hoarding useless information. But we'd hear him, or rather we'd hear his flip-flops as he walked out the back of the hooch on his way to the shower.

I'm not exactly sure what the bond between us was—the fact that we were both from small towns in Ohio, that our fathers worked in the tire industry, that we both canonized Jim Brown as the greatest football player of all time—whatever it was, Edwards and I were kinda tight, although I didn't want any of the other guys to know it because Edwards was, for them, a never ending source of derision.

"Who sat downwind of Qui Nhon today?" Richards would say whenever Edwards passed by. The guys referred to him as "the Boy from Qui Nhon City," blending his last assignment with the old Ad Libs' song "The Boy from New York City" to mock his personal hygiene.

"Jesus," Richards usually went on, "that guy needs to change his fucking fatigues one of these days!"

"You know what that dipshit told me today," Ward piped up. "He said that he'd personally corresponded with Hanoi Hannah and that she was really Nancy Kwan, the hot Asian actress who was on the cover of *Life*

Magazine back when we were thinking impure thoughts."

We all laughed, and didn't stop until we heard the flip-flop of Edwards' thongs.

"Evening, gents," he acknowledged us on his way back through the hooch. Richards hollered after him "Your fatigues were here a minute ago, looking for you. They need a bath too!"

Edwards didn't react. Funny thing was, he could have come down on us, outranking us all as he did, but there were more of us, and, well, sometimes bad shit went down.

* * *

No one knew that whenever I pulled guard duty, or got stuck with the overnight shift for the *Morning News Roundup*, I'd wake up to find Edwards in my cube, sitting on the edge of Moore's cot, thumbing through one of the many books I was reading. He had an especially hard time pronouncing the titles of Hermann Hesse novels.

Edwards would ask me about the plots and the characters. He was eager to learn more about *Magister Ludi,* the rite of passage in *Steppenwolf,* and Siddhartha's quest. I kinda enjoyed being the teacher and even looked forward to explaining the stories to him.

I didn't want the other guys to know.

That's because there were lots of not-so-great moments, times when Edwards did pull rank, when he felt that he had to remind us that he was in charge. The worst was the night he ratted us out to Lieutenant Nelson who paid a surprise visit to our hooch at 2 a.m. and subjected us to a fucking inspection. Shit, if any of us would have had access to a weapon that night—they took the guns away from us when we got off guard duty—somebody would've shot Edwards.

The SOB even had the gall to accompany Nelson on his hooch inspection, the two of them hoping like hell they'd catch us with our pants down, or more likely our pipes and pot out in the open. Why they never looked in the fridge, I don't know, but they didn't find squat. We knew the raid was Edwards's idea because it happened the day after Ward and a couple of other guys had swiped a pair of his fatigues, burned them, and put the ashes in his locker. Not to mention that Nelson, even though he was our direct command at the IO office, didn't even know where in the fuck we lived.

That incident made Edwards even more of a pariah with the guys, which explains why I'd only talk to him when nobody else was around. I was as pissed at him as anybody, but I lightened up after he gave me an authentic 1869 Cincinnati Red Stockings baseball cap. Edwards knew I loved baseball even more than writing, and almost as much as getting high.

* * *

"Do you write down what really happens or do you just write down what you're thinking and feeling?" I opened one eye on an early monsoon morning to see Edwards holding my copy of *The Tin Drum*.

"Whaddya mean?" I stretched out and put my feet on the cement floor.

"Are you writing a story or are you just keeping, like, a diary?"

"A little of both," I half-smiled. "A lot of what I write is about what I'm doing here and how much I hate this place and which one of my buddies is sleeping with my girlfriend back home." I paused. "Other times I read or hear about something that happened in country and I rewrite it, make a story out of it. Either way, I end up lost in my writing and forget I'm even in Vietnam."

"Can I read some of your stuff some time?" Edwards asked, sounding almost normal. I didn't know what to say. *Was this the same guy who was riding my ass just a few weeks ago?*

"I'd really like to read your stuff," he repeated. "I don't know a lot about writing but I've been reading a lot of books, and I could tell you what I think."

When I still didn't answer, Edwards reached across my bunk and put his hand on my arm. "Don't make me pull rank on you, son."

Fucking A, I thought to myself. *I don't owe Edwards shit, and I don't let anybody read my writing.* But then I got to thinking that Edwards could help me with the combat stuff I was always trying to write but knew next to nothing about.

Edwards kept looking at me.

"Let me think about it," I told him. He didn't look pleased, so of course I kept talking. "If I go for this, I make the rules and you follow them." *Where was I going with this?*

"Rule number one," I started. "Absolutely nobody, not a single swinging dick, knows we're doing this." Edwards nodded. "Rule number two—you do not touch a word, a punctuation mark, nothing. Hands off!" I paused.

"I've got a rule number three," he interjected. "Rule number three is you make sure the other guys go easy on me. I don't want to get into it with them because I might not be able to control myself."

* * *

Most of the shit I gave Edwards was short stories with
some occasional war reportage. I was trying to get into a
Hemingway groove but kept lapsing into Thomas Wolfe.
I never let Edwards read my journals. I didn't want him
knowing how insecure or scared or depressed I was.

For weeks Edwards read my stories, the ones about
guard duty and fraggings, the tales about Vietnamese
spies and the black market. Even the thinly disguised
ones about our office. He had some pretty good insights,
particularly about maintaining a character's voice or
how to show more and tell less.

What I wanted most was help writing about combat.
It was around us every day, it defined this whole fucking
war, but I'd never seen it. How could I capture its
violence, its cruelty, its insanity, its fickleness?

I handed Edwards my lone combat story one day, a
piece I'd written about a firefight. It was loosely based
on a bunch of stories I'd heard from grunts I'd interviewed and articles we'd run in *The Army Reporter*.

"Nobody I know talks like this," he told me the next
morning. "Nobody fights like this. Nobody dies like
this."

"Tell me how you really feel," I joked. My sarcasm
didn't register.

"I'll tell you what it was like for me," he offered, "and
you can try to write it into your story. It can't come out
any worse than this." He was serious.

I hesitated. "Okay, but you can't get pissed if I
change anything or have one of the story's characters
sound like you."

He sat stoically. "Have you ever read *The Art of War* by Sun Tzu?"

I didn't know what to say. Never in a million years would I have imagined someone like Edwards reading the famous book by an ancient Chinese military strategist.

"No, I haven't."

"You should," he replied earnestly. "It would help your writing about combat. In one place he says 'know your enemy and know yourself, and after a thousand battles you need never fear the result.'"

I looked right at him. "What the fuck does that have to do with anything?"

"Think about it," Edwards got up to leave.

* * *

For the next week, Edwards gave me a grunt's-eye primer on combat, always coming back to the same story about the same firefight, the "crack, crack, crack" of automatic weapons, his squad leader's legs being blown off, the guy next to him—Morgan I think his name was—standing up too soon and getting zapped right between his shoulder blades. Every night I'd write a new version. I never could get it right, never could capture the authenticity.

The whole exercise reminded me of my Intro to Philosophy class in college. We had this ancient professor with a droopy mustache who looked like he would have been at home in a toga. He loved talking about Plato and Plato's idea of a horse.

"Everything you see in a stable is really an imperfect representation of a form that exists in the ideal realm," he'd lecture us. Back then, all I could think about was the perfect coed body, but somehow the old professor's words stayed with me.

The professor-philosopher reminded us that one of Plato's critics told him that he "could see particular horses, but not horseness," to which Plato replied, "That's because you have eyes but no intelligence."

I had eyes, and ears, but when it came to combat, I lacked anything resembling intelligence. I had pen and paper, but I didn't have the story. I could write and write and write, but I'd never get it straight.

For me, Edwards's combat experience, hell, every grunt's combat experience was the ideal. I was stuck in the fucking cave with Plato.

In reality, the best I could do was pretend. So I kept on writing and distancing and putting myself to sleep.

* * *

I didn't have much luck getting the guys to lighten up on Edwards in the office or at the hooch. He didn't know when he was trying too hard or being an asshole. That was probably the lifer in him, the supply clerk. We draftees were better, purer. Plus we were educated and knew more than our bosses. As my uncle used to say, "we thought our shit didn't stink."

The best thing that happened to Edwards was Nixon and Vietnamization. Guys kept DEROS-ing and weren't being replaced, so our IO office numbers kept getting smaller and smaller, meaning there were fewer and fewer guys to pick on him. Eventually, it was just a handful of us, plus Miss Tran and Edwards, knocking out the publications and press releases that used to take dozens of us to produce. If nothing else, it made the time go fast.

The declining GI numbers gave me a chance to go out into the field in search of my combat story. Hard as I looked, I never found it. By this time, nobody wanted to be the last GI killed in Vietnam and no one was taking risks. The only real skirmish I saw was between South Vietnamese soldiers, ARVNs, and some grunts who thought the ARVN were a bunch of pussies. Their M-16s did make that "crack, crack, crack" sound that Edwards had described. And you really could smell danger in the air. Edwards hadn't lied.

One day I got back from one of those assignments and, lo and behold, Edwards was gone. Gone from Vietnam and out of the Army, too. None of the GIs left knew what happened or gave a flying fuck. Even Edwards himself didn't mention what happened in the letter he sent me.

"You were the only guy I could talk to at USARV," he wrote just before the end of my tour. *"I want to thank you for that. We needed all the friends we could get in 'Nam, and we were lucky to have each other. Maybe we'll meet up again someday. Liked your stories, Edwards."*

Inside the large manila envelope were photocopies of every one of my stories. My jaw dropped as I scanned his edits. They were meticulous. They were good. They were right. In a way, the stories were now more his than mine.

"You still writing that shit?" was the question Edwards posed to me that one morning in Vietnam. And as I sit here, light years away from that place, that time, and those people, the answer is "Yes, I'm still writing that   shit."

DEROS

As she slowly moved from the living room to the kitchen and back to the living room, stopping along the way to listen to the quiet which seemed to be getting louder, she realized that what was wrong was not something inside the apartment. It was inside her.

She gently massaged her stomach, then let her hand slide lower, to her uterus, to that area where she had housed him for nine months more than 22 years ago. That's where the pain was. It hurt like labor, but it was a different pain, a form of anti-labor, as if the doctor and nurses were opening her up and forcing her to take the afterbirth and the placenta and the cord back inside.

He was her baby. And he belonged there, if not inside her, then beside her, not in the car with his father, on the way to the airport and California and, all too soon, Vietnam.

What would they talk about in the car? she wondered. *Or would they talk at all?* She shook her head. How was it that these two, so much alike that it was sometimes painful to watch, had become prisoners of this Oedipal dance? And why did she, who knew each of their hurts and their fears, why did she have to mother both of them? Why did she have to mediate their anger and navigate their distance?

Would she ever see him again?

Which one, her mind quickly countered. As emotional as her husband was, he could easily succumb to a crying jag on the way home and drive right off the Schuylkill Expressway. And her son . . .

She paused as the aching in her womb struck back, pulling her stomach and her head and her heart with it.

DEROS? Was that the term he used? She envisioned the word in her head, storing it in her mind for a future crossword puzzle as she did with most new words she heard. But this one was made up, just another of those silly Army acronyms.

"What's a five letter word for the Greek God of . . . ?" *Of what?* she thought. Deliverance? Salvation? Reunion?

DEROS had something to do with return from overseas, but she couldn't remember the rest of it. The return from overseas was the important part. When would that be? When could they start counting down from 365? When would the pain go away?

As she reflected on "going away" she realized she was standing in front of the door to his bedroom. "Walk On By," she said aloud, pulling her hand back from the doorknob. She couldn't go in because she didn't want to face the disappointment of his not being there.

For a moment, she could still hear the music that he played so loud, especially the album that had the song "Walk On By" which so unnerved her. The voice of the black man in that song, his pleading, his hurt, all the longing in his voice, the female singers in the background, the electric guitar demanding to be heard.

Now she was inside his bedroom, fingering through the wooden crate next to his desk where he kept his record albums. She gasped, staring at what looked like a black baby's head emerging from the womb before she saw the sunglasses and the beads around the neck and realized it was the head of the black man who sang the song that took her son away and broke her heart.

She grabbed the copy of *Hot Buttered Soul* and tried first to break it, then bend it, with no success. There was only one thing left to do.

She opened the turntable, placed the album on the spindle, raised the needle and turned up the volume. Loud. Louder. An orchestra, violins—had they always been there? The guitar and then that deep, painful resonant voice, reminding her that she'd lost someone she loved.

Standing there, listening and crying, she knew what DEROS meant.

Malaria

The last order Master Sergeant Billy Taylor snapped as I left Fort Benning was: "Make sure y'all take these malaria pills 48 hours BEFORE you leave for 'Nam. Do you read me? If you don't do as I say, you'll get malaria and die 'fore you get sick of the fucking place."

Sgt. Taylor's words hovered above the dashboard as my dad maneuvered his VW bug through the rain and the Philadelphia rush-hour traffic. If it hadn't been for Sgt. Taylor's warning, my dad and I would be headed south toward the airport and my flights heading to the West coast and Southeast Asia. Instead, we were driving north—back home to fetch my forgotten malaria pills.

We approached my parents' apartment in silence. My dad pulled into the small circle in front of their building and turned off the ignition. I got out.

"I forgot my malaria pills," I told my mother as I returned to re-swell her puffy eyes and nose. Neither of us was up to a repeat of our previous, painful goodbyes. I grabbed the pills, pocketed them in the raincoat my dad gave me for protection, and kissed her between petrified tears.

Back on the road, my dad and I again sat in silence. Under normal circumstances, a hostile, damp night with tons of traffic and skittish drivers would throw him into a rage. Not tonight. He simply steered, coping with the demands of the highway, and my departure. As I watched him, I thought about how much we were alike, and how far we'd come in just 48 hours.

* * *

My parents were hosting a festive, pre, pre-Thanksgiving going-away dinner for me, accompanied by my girlfriend Emily.

"The Last Supper," I whispered to Emily, trying to explain all the familial hoopla.

My mother invited her sisters, Mae and Stella, and Stella's husband Joe, to join in the celebration. The seven of us dined on turkey and all the trimmings in front of the TV in the living room of my parents' tiny, two-bedroom apartment, watching the Oakland Raiders and Kansas City Chiefs play football.

Between first and second helpings, as I passed the gravy boat to Aunt Mae and joked about Thanksgiving in Vietnam, Aunt Stella and my dad leaped from their chairs and ran toward the TV. A skirmish had broken out between opposing linemen. Aunt Stella screamed: "Get the nigger! Get that nigger!" My father hollered, "Kill that black bastard!"

I exchanged a painful expression with Emily whose body visibly tightened. She was embarrassed for me, and I was angry with my family. In fact, on the 28th day of a 30-day, pre-Vietnam leave, I was pissed off about everything—my parents, Aunt Stella, racism, genocide, Nixon, Vietnam, Cambodia, Kent State, the draft—everything.

"What's your problem?" My father baited us, looking past me at Emily whom I suspected he already disliked. She hadn't responded to his good old boy flirting and hadn't laughed at one of his stupid jokes since she'd arrived.

"Back off, will you please, Dad?"

"It's my house; I can do as I please."

"Then try showing some consideration for people who don't share your prejudices."

Battle lines drawn, Emily quietly excused herself from the table while the rest of my relatives pretended to watch the football game.

"Don't hand me that high and mighty horseshit," my dad snarled. "I've had it up to here with your college-boy crap. You're no better than any of the rest of us. I was hoping the Army might change your attitude, but it hasn't. I'll guarantee you Vietnam will."

I glanced at my mom at the mention of "Vietnam." Her eyes moistened. I hated my father for upsetting her. I hated him for embarrassing me in front of Emily. I hated him for the war.

"Vietnam will straighten you out," he continued. "You mark my words. Do you good to defend this great country."

"TOUCHDOWN!" Aunt Stella shrieked. I shook my head, swallowed my words and left to look for Emily. She wasn't in the guest bedroom. She wasn't on the balcony either.

I walked down the narrow hallway to my parents' bedroom. Even though they always turned the heat in their apartment up way too high, my folks usually kept the large windows in their back bedroom wide open. The pitch-black room was cool, almost cold, like a cave hidden away among the nearby Pocono Mountains.

I thought I heard something when I entered the room, but I was so exhausted that I collapsed on my parents' firm, queen-sized bed. It was then that I detected the sound of another person's breathing. The rhythm of the barely audible sighs told me that it was Emily. We didn't talk about what had just happened, or what was going to happen in less than 48 hours.

"Do you remember that turkey dinner I cooked for you and your Army buddies last summer in your apartment?" mused Emily. "Not nearly as good as your mom's food. I worked all day on that meal and then that asshole roommate of yours—Frank—joked about how he couldn't eat a turkey dinner if it wasn't Thanksgiving and hadn't been made by a family member of his—he kept rubbing it in all night—you didn't stop him. What a jerk he was. I never liked that guy."

Emily kept going on like that, never pausing to ask me for an answer. She needed to let down, and the cool, dark quiet was helping her to do that.

After a while I started to talk to the darkness myself.

"I've been looking for an answer to why I'm bound for Vietnam," I began. "First, I thought I was some sort of innocent victim, a casualty of life's unfairness. Then I decided it was fate. But that didn't make any sense either, especially for a good Catholic boy like me.

"Next, I thought it was punishment for something bad I'd done—a sin I'd forgotten to confess, some wrong that I didn't bother to right. Later, I turned to astrology, then Tarot cards, marijuana, meditation, more dope, the Grateful Dead—none of it worked.

"Then it hit me—it was my parents' fault!"

Was Emily listening? She seemed to still be breathing in the cool night air and breathing out her anxiety.

"It is their fault, goddamn it. I mean, shit, I made it to the draft lottery, which was going to save my ass. But the day before my birthday was picked out of the fucking fishbowl as number two-fifty something. And the day after was three sixty-six! Are you shitting me? But my birthday! Number nine! Fuck, I might as well have packed my bags for Vietnam the day I was born."

We both lay there, Emily replaying the weeks we'd spent together before tonight, our final night, while I continued to make a case against my parents for their lousy family planning. I needed so bad for someone, for Emily, to hold me right then. But I didn't reach across the bed. I wanted her to find me, to caress me, to comfort me.

Lost in our respective monologues, Emily and I were unaware that the bedroom door had opened and a crack of light from the hallway reaffirmed how dark it was.

Someone had entered the room. Neither of us moved. I wasn't frightened because I knew it was my dad. And when he lay down on the bed between us, it seemed inexplicably natural.

"It broke my mother's heart when I went into the service," he recalled softly, almost privately. The hostility was gone from his voice. Emily and I stopped our own musings and listened to his whispered memories.

"But it wasn't my mother, or yours, who was hurt the most, or frightened the most, by what I had to do," he continued, "it was me. Did I ever tell you what an unheroic fellow your father was? It was late 1943, almost 1944—Nineteen Forty-Four!—before I joined the Army! Did I enlist? Did I run down to my local recruiting station and sign up to kick Hitler and Hirohito's butts? No. I had to be drafted. The end of 1943 and the world was going to hell and I had to be drafted."

None of us moved. We were floating through space and time on a bed in a bedroom in an apartment in a city somewhere between Pearl Harbor and Saigon.

"They had to come and get me," my dad admitted. "Sure, I wanted to beat the Japs and the Nazis. But I was scared to death. I didn't want to die. I didn't want to have to kill someone. I didn't want to go. I didn't want to fight. And now," he paused, nearly choking on his words. "And now, twenty-five years later, my son has to do the same goddamn thing—only this time it's worse. He's gotta do something that nobody in his right mind wants to do for a country that's not sure whether he should be doing it, in a place that nobody can pronounce the same way.

"And . . ." he hesitated. "And . . . it's all my fault."

Was Emily listening? My mother? My father's mother?

"It's all my fault because I got mad and I got lazy," my dad's voice seemed stronger. "I got mad at my son because he was telling me things I didn't want to hear. And I got lazy because I believed everything my country was telling me. I believed in every damn thing we were doing everywhere. I believed. And now—in return—I have to give them my son."

He stopped, drawing a deep breath that pulled me and Emily and the darkness in with it.

* * *

I'm not sure how long we three silently lay there. Maybe an hour. Or a lifetime. But that moment has given way to this, the one that finds us on the way to the airport, and my eventual arrival in Vietnam.

Driving in the same confessional silence that we'd shared two nights before, I knew I loved my father and always would. But in our new communion, I forgot about the malaria pills I'd tucked inside his raincoat.

Insubordination Nation

Their morning ritual. Her paper. His paper. Her news. His sports.

Maybe this is what Simon & Garfunkel meant by the "sounds of silence?" Her tsks, a-hems and phews; his head shaking from side to side.

As with every news nugget she uncovered daily, his wife broke the quiet.

"How come an Army reserve officer is facing insubordination charges?" Her question wrenched him away from his daily homage to Seattle Mariners' statistics. Any time there was the slightest article or mention of military justice, she turned to him as the ultimate authority. Little did she know that he had left all that behind, far far behind and that he could care less about the Uniform Code of Military Justice.

"It says here," she continued, her gray hair falling over her eyes and diving into her bowl of Special K, "that Captain Steve McAlpin of the 401st Civil Affairs Battalion questioned the legality of a waiver that his battalion was asked to sign allowing their third deployment to a war zone since January."

"Waiver?" she directs the question squarely at him, and then returns to the Associated Press article. "He was then notified in a memorandum Wednesday that he was being removed from the unit's battle roster and that he could face additional punishment, including a court-martial and losing rank, over the charges."

She swept her hair from her eyes for the umpteenth time.

"I mean, can they really do this to a guy who's a citizen soldier?" she begged. "If they're receiving memos and signing waivers, then aren't reservists different than common soldiers?"

More annoyed with the fact his beloved Mariners were 20 games above .500 but still eight games behind the first place Athletics, he reached over and grabbed the article.

"A spokesman for the 401st," he read as if he were delivering a commencement address, mainly to piss off his wife, "said Friday that McAlpin's questioning of the waiver was one reason why he was being disciplined. Individual members of the 401st are allowed to refuse to sign the waiver, but the spokesman said McAlpin was 'butting in' for other soldiers."

Now his voice was sing-songing. "There's lots of soldiers we're not sending because they have one issue or another," the spokesman added. "It's important we put together a solid team. Not all soldiers are ready, even though they think they are, to deploy.

"McAlpin, a twenty-five-year military veteran, told the *Rochester Democrat and Chronicle* that instead of signing the reprimand document, he attached a note of protest, stating his performance evaluations have been excellent and that his record shows 'no pattern of incompetence.' He also plans to meet with a military attorney."

His wife sat, waiting for his explanation, for his insight into the intricacies of military justice. It never came.

His eyes locked on that last line: "He also plans to meet with a military attorney," and he vaguely recalled a similar plea from a platoon of soldiers stationed at Fort

Dix, New Jersey, in early 1970. Something to do with a protest and a Beatles song?

Happiness is a Warm Gun? he wondered.

He never did get involved with that case, but he couldn't recall why he didn't. Besides, his participation wouldn't have changed a fucking thing. Some guys got court-martialed, some went to the brig, some went AWOL, and some got killed. McAlpin had better realize that the Army held all the cards and his ass was theirs.

Now, what was Ichiro's batting average again?

Basic Choices

Dear Lamont:

Man, I hate like hell to lay this on you, but I've been drafted by the rest of the guys to write and ask your advice. Even though I'm crunched for time and we aren't even sure this letter will reach you at home before you head off to Fort Lee and your legal specialist training, I'm going to give it a try. As our resident b-ball star Robinson likes to say "Son, you miss all the shots you never take!"

I can't remember exactly when you came down with mono and they moved you out. Four, five weeks ago? I know you were here for Easter Sunday dinner because my parents drove up from Pottstown, and I remember their saying nice things about the "charming Negro" from Newark. At that point, I'm pretty sure we hadn't started "weapons familiarization." Yeah, that's about when you left, before the firing started.

Anyway, when this shit storm hit, everybody said, "Go tell Lamont what went down and he'll figure out how to deal with all this." So, Lamont Dozier, you've been selected by a jury of your peers to be our eyes, our ears, and, we're hoping, our brains.

What we did the other night is related, I'm not sure just how, to the fact that we were minus Sgt. Cannon, our DI, the final few weeks of basic training. That's my view at least—too much fucking freedom of choice. Jesus, the Army's calling what happened an "organized mutiny" or "planned insurrection" if you can believe that. I'll just lay out the facts and let you be the judge.

A few days after Easter, Sgt. Cannon got his orders to return to Vietnam. Can you believe that? The goddamn guy had been there twice already, owns a wall full of medals and a Purple Heart, not to mention having a wife and two kids. And he volunteered to go back to fucking 'Nam. He told us it had something do to with "repaying debts" and giving the South Vietnamese the "freedom to choose." You remember his rap about democracy and loyalty and commitment? Christ, I'll bet a guy with your smarts could repeat that speech of his word for word.

The day Sgt. Cannon got his orders, he was on our floor in the barracks, consoling my bunkmate Collins (remember Collins from Aliquippa?) about picking up a gun. Collins had been fretting about this for weeks and had sought advice and counsel from just about everybody at Fort Dix, including the company chaplain—and even the local rabbi—about his not wanting to carry, or fire, a weapon.

The weird thing was that it was Cannon, the highly-decorated, gung-ho, "grab 'em by the balls and their hearts and minds will follow" soldier who was the most sympathetic to Collins. We don't know what he said or how he did it, but Cannon helped Collins to deal with the gun thing and to get through that part of basic training. We all can use a guy like Cannon in our corner.

So, here we were, "50 characters without an author" as Doc O'Brien called us (not that any of us knew what he meant by that), waist-deep in weapons familiarization and without Sgt. Cannon or any other assigned drill instructor! I mean, the Army was breaking its own rules by not having someone bunk with us and ride herd, but I guess they were short-handed because we went through the next few weeks—everything from shot grouping to zeroing to hand grenades to initial tactical training—on our own. Sure, the other company DIs kicked our butts when we were training and what have you, but nobody was with us non-stop from reveille to lights out.

We were into the last phase of the Field Exercises, and you just knew the whole fucking schedule was off because of all the rain and mud and Cannon's leaving and how uptight all the DIs and brass were. They needed more cannon fodder for their fucking war and here we were stuck in the mud in New Jersey!

We'd already completed the 15K foot march after our first trip out to Poorman's Range, so they decide to take us out and back to TT6 Night Infiltration in cattle cars so we'd get back to the base at a reasonable hour. Jesus, those goddamn cattle cars were just that—and we were the friggin cattle. There we were, 50 wet, muddy, and pissed-off newbies crammed into this large, mobile box on wheels, minus a damn drill sergeant.

You and I first met on one of those cattle cars, remember? Fresh out of reception, we gathered all 70 pounds of the finest Government Issue equipment and hustled on so we wouldn't get our asses kicked. You didn't want to be last, or be caught looking lost or sad. I remember there was one guy crying and man did they let that wimp have it!

Yeah, I can still remember them cramming in as many of us as humanely possible and then Senior Drill Sergeant Torres came on board and read us the riot act. All we could do was hang our heads and ride in silence to our new home at Fort Dix.

You figured out right away that we were driving around in circles so that the Army could mess with our heads and let the reality of belonging to them and being in the military sink in. Maybe that's why we acted up like we did later on and sang the song we sang. All of us, every last one of us, had come to own that sinking feeling of being pushed down, down, down by Uncle Sam.

Anyway, what a fucking sight we were after our inglorious night infiltration. A goddamn cattle car full of Charles Schultz's Pigpens but without the dust—we were filthy, wet, and muddy. Tired. Pissed. Doomed. Our fucking driver was obviously pissed off, taking the turns on the route back to the barracks at way more than 40 miles an hour. GIs were being tossed from one side of the car to the other; guys were falling on top of each other, screaming, cursing. I was waiting for some fight to break out. I was especially watching for Murphy, because, as you know, he'd had it in for me from day one, threatening he'd stick me when I least expected it. Lucky for me, he was on the bottom of a pile that included Denny "Haystacks" Calhoun and Myron "Bubba" Brown. Needless to say, Murphy wasn't going anywhere.

That's how things looked from my spot in the middle of the car, where I was hanging on for dear life to Collins who was holding on to one of the poles that ran from floor to ceiling. It was probably worse if you were one of the guys on the bottom of the pile, or if you were wetter and muddier than I was. Remember that line of Thoreau's you used to always recite to us about most men living lives of quiet desperation? We had it half right. We were desperate, but loud and angry, too.

We all fucking knew that when we got back to the barracks, even as late as it was, we'd be ordered to formation, then made to clean our weapons and return them before we'd get to bed. Christ, it would be two in the fucking morning before we'd get to sleep. You could just sense that every last "swinging dick," as Sgt. Cannon used to call us when he came through the barracks to wake us in the morning, had had it with the Army and basic training and Vietnam and everything and was about ready to explode.

That was when Doc and the Professor started singing "Yellow Submarine." I'm not sure why that song or what it had to do with anything. Maybe it was on account of we were all feeling submerged somehow, both by the rain and the mud, and by the Army and Vietnam, too.

Doc began singing the first line, his voice sounding purer and clearer than I ever remember it being any time during basic training. Man, he had some pipes, and he was sounding so, well, so grown-up.

The Professor joined in on the next line of the song, his voice a little deeper and fuller than Doc's. Funny that it was the two oldest guys in our platoon, and the only two college graduates beside you, who were doing the singing because they'd always kept a low profile.

Suddenly, it got quiet in the cattle car. For all I know we were still careening around corners and banging into one another, but we all started listening to them, as their voices go louder. When they finally got to the chorus, Doc banged the butt of his M-16 on the floor of the cattle car for emphasis. It made a great sound, a perfect thump/clang and, spontaneously, every last one of us was banging our M-16s on the floor to emphasize every "yellow submarine" utterance.

I can't really describe for you what it was like being caught up in that moment. We all felt alive and somehow liberated, as if we weren't any longer in the Army or stuck in Fort Dix, New Jersey. Somehow we'd been transported to some other time, some better place, where bands played and people got along and sang songs and had fun.

In our reverie, we'd lost track of just how fast the cattle car was moving and arrived back at our company headquarters, the entire cattle car belting out "Yellow Submarine" at top volume. The guys at headquarters must have known we were coming for miles because we were singing really loud.

Finally, Charles heard the banging on the side door and opened it, only to encounter a very pissed-off Master Sergeant Willie Brown and First Lieutenant Cory Watkins staring him in the face. Oddly, Charles didn't shout "ten-hut" or anything. He just greeted them warmly and said, "Come right in."

This nonchalant welcome made Brown and Watkins madder. They ordered us to stop singing, which we did, but we kept banging our M-16s on the floor of the cattle car. It sounded like a minor earthquake. It was hard to hear everything they were saying, but I was able to pick out parts of it. They accused us of being insubordinate, told us we were guilty of gross disciplinary infractions, and that the Army would deal harshly by giving us all an Article 15.

They also called us names, like jerk-offs and douche bags. After a while, their putdowns reminded me of the parents in "Bye, Bye Birdie" who complained about their kids being "disobedient, disrespectful oafs."

That's how I started playing their taunts in my head. It was a movie, and they were challenging us for being "*noisy, crazy, dirty, lazy loafers.*"

"*You can talk and talk till your face is blue,*" Brown and Watkins seemed to harmonize, "*but they still just do what they want to do.*"

Yep, I was singing to myself, *"why can't they be like we were/lifers in every way/what's the matter with draftees today?"*

You knew something would have to give and that somebody, us, was going to have to pay for this, but for that one brief moment, we had them by the balls because we'd fucked up their schedule and done something they didn't expect us to do. Hell, if they would have thought about it for a minute and gotten over being pissed, Brown and Watkins might have realized that they'd accomplished their mission with us—we were acting as a team, not as individuals. We were singing and protesting, but we'd come together as a group which was the whole fucking objective of basic training, no?

They told us our punishment would be three-fold. First, after we got our asses off the cattle car, we'd stand in formation, at attention, in complete silence, for an hour. Then we'd hand over our M16s without cleaning them and do a forced march back to our barracks.

After that trek, we'd return to reclaim our weapons—and then clean them—at 0400 hours. Meaning, of course, we'd get all of about two hours of sleep before we'd have to pack up and head out for the company's 10K footmarch to the bivouac site for our final field training exercise.

To top it off, at the upcoming graduation ceremony, as everybody else in the company would be presented their Army insignia and mementos by their Drill Sergeants, we'd be served with our Article 15s. In front of our friends and family, no less.

That's when it hit all of us that we needed you! You know as much about military law as anyone—you used to repeat that funny Groucho Marx line "Military justice is to justice as military music is to music" —and Collins says you're planning to go to law school some day. Plus, everybody remembered those late-night "legal seminars" you used to hold, the ones where you told us about Article 15 of the Uniform Code of Military Justice and Part V of the Manual for Courts-Martial. In other words, you woke us all up to the fact that when it came to law and authority, the Army was holding all the cards.

"An Article 15 gives a commanding officer power to punish individuals for minor offenses," you explained, pointing out that the term "minor offense" was a source for concern in the administration of nonjudical punishments. But, as you reminded us, the final determination as to whether an offense is minor, and I quote (I even wrote this down), "is within the sound discretion of the commanding officer."

In fact, my brother, you might have taught us too well. Doc claims you opened his eyes to a loophole in the entire process which is why we're having this debate. According to Doc, "Subsection (a) of Section 815, Article 15 of the Commanding Officer's Non-judicial Punishment regs states that Article 15s may not be imposed upon any member of the armed forces under this article if the member has, before the imposition of such punishment, demanded trial by court-martial in lieu of such punishment."

If he's right, some of us think that if all 50 of us were to choose a court-martial instead of an Article 15, we could really fuck the Army up. Shit, they would have to hold individual court-martial proceedings for each of us, and it would cost them a shitload of time and money.

Of course, the counterargument—and more of the guys are on this side—is that if we even dared to this, the

Army would really fuck us over. They'd probably apply a different definition to "minor offense" and try us by general court-martial, meaning we all could receive dishonorable discharges or get locked up. Where the fuck's Perry Mason when you need him? Probably in his office making time with the lovely Della Street.

Lamont, the guys asked me to write and get your opinion on the Article 15-court-martial question, but I'm guessing it's too late for that. Regardless of what we decide to do, we know that they'll throw the book at us. At a minimum we'll all be made 11 Bravos once this is done. Which means we'll all be in 'Nam within four months and some of us won't be coming home.

But that's not why I'm writing. Don't tell the rest of them, but I'm writing because I need you to tell me if any of this makes a goddamn difference. I mean, if we'd raised our voices sooner, and louder, if we'd joined in with other GIs who were, would that have made a difference? Changed anything?

I'm not asking you if we did the right thing with our "Yellow Submarine" stunt, but I'm asking if what we did is really enough? And if it isn't, what can we do, what choices do we have, if we want to change the way things are going? If we want to save a life, say Sgt. Cannon's life?

Have we deluded ourselves into thinking that we had any choice at all?

Sorry for the long letter and all the heavy questions. We're meeting with our defense counsel in a few minutes. Some young JAG officer from Manchester, New Hampshire. Hope he likes the Beatles.

Peace,
Rick

Race Against Time

Once upon a time they called him Aubrey Moore. That was the slave name he inherited, growing up in Valdosta, Georgia, USA, where he was shown his place and stayed put.

Head down. Eyes lowered.

Dr. Martin Luther King, Jr. once won second prize in a high school oratory contest in Valdosta. Aubrey's English teacher remembered King's being there, and told Aubrey's class how the young Reverend's voice fillied the halls, his words piercing the quiet classrooms like a warrior's sword.

Now King was dead.

And so was Aubrey Moore.

Malik Hekalu (Translation: King Temple) was who he was, rising from the jungles of Southeast Asia, a mixture of Arabic and Swahili. Muslim and African. King, servant no more.

Malik demonstrated his new station every day in Vietnam by the ritual greeting he gave his brothers. It started with eye contact, then slight hand contact, and suddenly a flurry of rapid gestures—a complicated routine of shakes, slaps, snaps, grips, and bumps familiar only to Malik and his greeter.

Four black hands in constant motion—slapping, snapping, wiggling fingers, mutual knuckle bumps, and ever so slight finger waves.

Black GIs called it dapping. White soldiers said the term DAP was an acronym that stood for "dignity and pride," mimicking the black power movement back in the world. Malik and his brothers laughed at this and said it was a "blackronym," an explanation thought up by whites after the fact.

Truth is, if you watched, if you listened, you could actually hear the message in a dap greeting—anything from *life is good* to *shit is fucked up here* to *you better watch your ass.* The pulling of the slightly cupped hands of the greeting participants against each other would send echoes across the base.

Malik Hekalu dapped his way through the rest of his tour in Vietnam. He even taught some of the Vietnamese how to dap. They told Malik that *dap* sounded like the Vietnamese word for beautiful. The women especially thought he was beautiful.

Which is why he decided to walk away from the Army and hang out with the Vietnamese who referred to him as *Midan*, or black man.

With them, he was able to be Malik. He loved being Malik. And he always talked with his hands, his strong, swift, black hands.

One day he started telling the story of the scores of African Americans from his hometown of Valdosta—farmers, craftsmen, and cotton pickers—who had left Georgia in the 1850s and 1860s for a better life in Liberia, Africa.

Telling that story to the Vietnamese took Malik a long, long time.

Ticket to Soulville

Dwight Johnson held tightly to his father's right arm at the elbow. Tethered this way, the two men meandered through a display of photos, letters, and military artifacts. Dwight's attempt to steer his father through the exhibit served to steady them both. He hadn't realized until now how skeletal his father's arm was, that there were fragments of something, maybe bone, floating around underneath his skin at the elbow.

"Pops, slow down," he said almost sweetly to his father. Reggie Johnson kept right on walking, eyes locked straight ahead. His son quickened his pace to stay with him.

"We need to stay with the rest of the group, Pops." Dwight was directing his voice to his father's good ear. He gestured toward a cluster of folks—the tour group they came with—standing at ease behind them, a mix of old and young, large and small, firm and infirm. People of all shades, from beige to brown to black.

A distinguished-looking man with a thick mustache, crisp white shirt, and bright bow tie was pointing to a military jacket that hung behind a plate of glass. Dwight escorted his father back to the group, his arm again pressed at the elbow. He felt his father flinch at the pressure.

"This is a Marine poncho-jacket," the bow-tied tour guide explained. "It was worn by a decorated Marine named James Anthony who served two Vietnam tours of duty between 1967 and 1969. I want you to notice the personal embroidery over the breast pocket. Can anyone see what it says?"

Silence. Until now, they'd only shared whispers, afraid if they raised their voices they might raise the spirits of dead soldiers, or resurrect buried memories.

"No one knows what this brother is talkin' 'bout?" The guide's lapse into vernacular elicited a ripple of laughter. A tall young man in the back, his baseball cap turned backward and his t-shirt sporting an image of the rapper Ludacris, raised his hand.

"It says 'black and proud.' It's a shout out to James Brown's hit song 'Say it Loud, I'm Black and I'm Proud' that was huge in the late '60s. My granddaddy was in Vietnam around that time. Said he saw James Brown in person!"

"You and your grandpa will have to tell us more about that later," the guide smiled and signaled the group to move along. "James Brown's trip to Vietnam comes up several more times in this exhibit."

"What'd he say?" Reggie asked Dwight, a mixture of frustration and alarm in his voice. "What did Mr. Lewis just say?"

"He was talking about the Marine's poncho," he shouted into his father's right ear, "and about James Brown's performing for troops in Vietnam."

"Entertaining," his father shot back, almost defiant-ly. "James Brown might have entertained white GIs. He performed for us brothers."

Before he could ask for clarification, Dwight realized the young man with the Ludacris t-shirt was standing next to them. His two hands rested on the back of a wheelchair where a white-haired man sat, looking intently at his father.

"Ain't that the truth, brother," the white-haired gen-tleman said, his voice raspy. "Hell, if they hadn't talked James Brown into going to Vietnam, the shit would have really hit the fan." The old man's eyes jumped as he spoke, punctuating his sentences. He stretched his hand upward toward Reggie's.

"Earl Floyd," he offered, "1968-69." As Earl's hand drew near Reggie's, it began to dip and snap and crack in what looked to Dwight like a sorcerer's wave.

"Reggie Johnson, Monkey Mountain, 1967-68," his father replied. Dwight and the younger man watched dumbfounded as Reggie returned the smacking and snapping and various hand gestures.

"Camp Tien Sha," Reggie smiled at Earl. "You there with the Mau Mau Brothers." Less question than statement.

Earl nodded. Dwight felt as if he was eavesdropping on something he shouldn't. A quick glance at Ludacris t-shirt confirmed that he shared the same feeling.

"That's what makes this exhibit so important," Earl spoke loud enough for Reggie, and probably the rest of the group, to hear. "Most folks don't know nothin' about what brothers had to deal with in Vietnam." He paused and brushed the hand that rested on the top of his wheelchair. "This is my grandson Sharif."

Heads nodded all around.

"We come down from Pittsburgh. That's where all this," Earl waved at the exhibit, "started out. Interest was so high at the Heinz History Center that they put a travelin' show together last year. Been to Dallas, Philadelphia, Richmond, Chicago, and Birmingham."

"And now Memphis," Sharif volunteered. Earl threw him a look that said *mind your manners.*

"It's not about the firefights and battles," Earl continued. "It's a whole damn history of Black, with a capital B."

Both Dwight and Sharif tensed up at the term black-ness.

"You remember that brother wrote for *Time* or *Life* or one of them? Wallace Terry. He called the frontlines 'Soulville.'" Reggie's head nods accelerated as Earl spoke. "Told some truth about how we brought that back home. People talk about the Panthers and Malcolm. All that grew up right there in Vietnam."

Earl stopped suddenly as he and the others became aware that the men and women in the group ahead of them were asking questions about Wallace Terry. The next section of the exhibit was dedicated to the man Earl was talking about.

Drawing closer, they saw an old manual typewriter, a camera, photographs, magazine stories, Black Power flags, and copies of *Bloods*, Terry's oral history about black soldiers in Vietnam.

"Why did these soldiers have their own flags?" asked a slight, middle-aged woman.

The guide looked directly at Earl and Reggie. "I think we have a couple gentlemen here who can shed some light on that."

Reggie felt like running and hiding. Earl rested his hand on Reggie's wrist, looked him in the eye, and smiled.

"It was about who we were, our identity." Earl offered. "The good Reverend Doctor King referred to the Vietnam War as a white man's war but a black man's fight. When they shot him down," he paused, "happened right down the street from here." Dwight recalled the shame and anger he felt for that moment in his hometown's history. "Some white soldiers in Vietnam celebrated by burning crosses, putting on Klan costumes, and flying the Confederate flag."

The woman who asked the question groaned. Earl reached out his hand to console her.

"Thank you," the guide said to Earl as he nodded to Dwight's father. "As I said at the start, this exhibit is a social tapestry of how the Civil Rights Movement paralleled the experience of the Black soldiers. *Soul on Ice, The Autobiography of Malcolm X,* sayings like 'Right On' and 'Solid.' It was all there in Vietnam."

Dwight turned to look at his father. For an instant, he saw himself in Reggie's face. And his grandfather, Carl, who worked as a janitor in a library while Reggie was overseas in Vietnam. Then it hit him.

"Pops," he murmured in Reggie's good ear. "Pops . . . " Reggie looked directly into Dwight's eyes. "The stick, the one in your bedroom all these years. . . " Dwight paused, afraid to go any further. Reggie closed his eyes and his face tightened before he opened them and embraced his son.

Dwight and Reggie froze, while Earl, Sharif and the others moved on to the next part of the exhibit, a recreated Vietnam barracks filled with footlockers, C-rations, stereo equipment, flags, and posters.

"Next, we'll see how some soldiers began demanding Black-only hooches, or barracks, which were sometimes referred to as *hekula*, the Swahili word for temple," the guide's voice trailed off. "Black GIs also created elaborate bootlace bracelets, which some called slave shackles, as a sign of solidarity."

Holding his father's arm, Dwight conjured the vision of the gnarled piece of wood that stood in the corner of Reggie and Pearl's bedroom at home. His father's walking stick was really his Vietnam salvation. Dwight recited in his head the names carved on it that stick, what he knew now as the names of every black soldier who had joined Reggie's unit in Vietnam.

Johnson. Smith. McNeil. Bradley. Moore. Bell. Simmons. Allen.

"Say it loud," Dwight hugged his father, directing those words into Reggie's shoulder. "I'm black and I'm proud."

Postcard from Hell

"Fuck 'em," the scowling soldier muttered under his breath as he got off the military bus at MACV headquarters. *They think they're so bad ass, riding in cyclos and expensive taxis over to TuDo Street where they'll spend all their hazardous duty pay on Saigon teas and cheap whores.* He was still smarting from being abandoned by his buddies, who obviously preferred the company of ladies to joining him for a walking tour of the Saigon of his idol, Graham Greene.

"When they get their hearts broken," he said aloud to no one in particular, "or better yet, when they get the clap, I'll be the one who's smiling."

He was standing in front of the legendary Majestic Hotel on Rue Catinat, just down the street from the Continental Palace Hotel. The Palace was where all the lazy-ass correspondents hung out because that's where they thought Greene had written his greatest book, *The Quiet American*. But understanding Greene as he did, he knew they were wrong because an upper-crust dude like Greene would much prefer the opulent Majestic to the trendy Palace.

And what a jewel the Majestic Hotel was! Tucked away from the noise and dangers of Rue Catinat, it housed a cool central courtyard, a ridiculous pool, and an amazing rooftop bar. He recalled standing up there one of his first nights in Saigon when the fucking Army wasn't sure if he was supposed to be stationed at MACV or USARV.

Soaking in the heat and the sounds and the smells of Saigon that evening, he pretended he was the all-knowing Camera Eye in John Dos Passos' *USA Trilogy*. Zooming in, he could see everything up and down the Saigon River. In those few moments, he knew all there was to know about this city, the country, and the fucked-up war. Graham Greene knew that, too, because he had stood up there and seen the same things.

He walked a little further up the Rue Catinat to the Palais Cafe, where Thomas Fowler had played *quatre cent vingt-et-un* with Lieutenant Vigot of the *Sûreté*. The bar was crowded, so he headed down the street to apartment 109 where Greene had once lived. There was nobody home.

Reluctantly, he made his way to the Continental Hotel because he knew he had to include it in his tour. Sure enough, it was stuffed with journalists from all over the USA and almost every country you could imagine, getting drunk, pretending to be part of some heavy political intrigue. He remembered Greene himself saying that the Continental had a slightly more traditional Vietnamese feel than the distinctly French-influenced Majestic and Grand. The outdoor bar spilled over with would-be authors and make-shift spies. Modern day Fowlers rendezvousing with their Pyles.

He paused, knowing that if he went any further he'd be too close to his buddies, near the place the French called "Le Parc au Buffles," which Greene had dubbed "The House of 500 Girls." Not far from there, off to the left, stood his greatest temptation, the place he knew he'd eventually wind up. He could hear strains of "96 Tears" amid the din of wheels rumbling over wooden floors. He could smell the opium. He could feel the high. He would go no further.

He knew he would never be a great author. He knew he would never get the story of Vietnam straight. He knew he didn't have the language to explain anything about any of this.

But, as he sat down at his usual table in the rear of the room and begin to pull on his pipe, he started feeling the old, enjoyable sensation. "A gradual, creeping thrill," is how one of the den's patrons described it. The anticipation was almost as good as the high itself.

The smoke spread through his body, painting him in pleasure from head to toe. It was in this state that he'd take out his pen and write another of his postcards home.

"Weather's fine, wish you were here," he'd begin. "It's such a magical time in Vietnam right now. Hand-to-hand combat is way down, the black market is up, and the dollar is strong. If you want to see Vietnam while its charm is still fresh, now is the time! Flak jackets are optional."

The Quiet Americans

I'm one of those maladjusted vets you're always hearing about. Been through a string of jobs and girlfriends. Drink too much. Edgy. Can't stand it when people order me around.

Charlie's just the opposite. He's my best buddy from 'Nam, and it's as if he hadn't ever been in the goddamn place. Hell, he comes back home to the missus, lands a good fucking job just like that, has a couple kids, buys a house, and, presto, he's right back in the mainstream.

Charlie and I pledged to talk on the phone every week and be there for one another, but we'd drifted apart a little. That's why I made a special point of stopping off in Kansas City for a few hours during one of my trips between the coasts. It was almost the second anniversary of our return to the world.

He and I had spent an entire year—365 days on the button—together in Vietnam. We were statewide together for six months prior to that. You could say that we had served the same sentence.

Besides, I liked Charlie. I could talk to him.

I was surprised when Charlie said he'd meet me at the airport and not at his house. He didn't give his reasons, so I cooled my heels at the terminal and waited for him.

"Rick," Charlie greeted me, extending his hand.

"Charlie," I shouted, holding back the hug I usually give him.

"How's Diane?" he asked.

"Deborah," I corrected him. "She's okay," I lied.

Charlie fidgeted. "Where the hell are you going from here?"

"Chicago. I've got about three hours. What's going on?

"You wouldn't believe it," Charlie said, slowly shaking his head. "You just would not fucking believe it."

Normally, this was my line. Charlie never swore.

"Try me," I volunteered.

"Let's go sit down somewhere," he said, motioning toward one of those nondescript airport fern bars.

The bar wasn't very crowded this time of day. We walked toward the rear of the narrow room, seeking out the most remote seats.

"What the hell is it, Charlie? Something with Cathy and the kids?"

"No, no," he waved me off. "It's crazier than that."

I sat back, took a deep breath and tried to prepare myself. I looked over at the table nearest us and noticed four Asians huddled together. Vietnamese. Ever since my tour of duty in South Vietnam, I'd been able to tell them from Chinese or Japanese. Shit, I can actually tell a Vietnamese from a Hmong or a Cambodian.

"You remember Tom Nevin?" I nodded. "Well, I got this out-of-nowhere call from him a couple months ago. He was having a blowout party 'cause he was leaving Boston and the *Globe* to head west to work for some new weekly in Colorado.

"Anyway, he begs me to come up to the party. Says he tried contacting you but your phone was disconnected . . ."

"Bullshit," I interrupted. "Nevin knows how the fuck to get a hold of me. He didn't try. He likes you better. Always has."

Charlie didn't go for the bait. "I broke my butt to get up there," he continued. "It was one wild party. I have never seen anybody drink more than those newspaper reporters, except for us at the USARV IO hooch."

A commotion arose at the next table. Our Vietnamese comrades were arguing over what looked like diaries or journals laid on the table. My Vietnamese was so rusty that I couldn't really make out what they were saying, except for an occasional "Bac Si" and "Dien Cai Dau."

"Finally, it's almost four in the morning and Nevin and I are sitting in some god-awful Worcester bar," Charlie continued, oblivious to the disturbance at the nearby table. "Then Nevin pulls his typical 'wasted at 4 a.m.' stunt—you might remember this from his DEROS party at Long Binh—champagne and popcorn. We were both completely out of it by then."

I couldn't take my eyes off the Vietnamese. The argument was really heating up. Something to do with the images in the diaries. By now, I was almost certain I recognized one of them from Vietnam. USARV headquarters? MACV in Saigon? Or was he the guy who ground the lenses for my granny glasses?

"Rick" Charlie grabbed me hard by the arm. "For Christ fucking sake, Rick, this is important!"

His voice surprised me. There was something in it I'd never heard before.

"After some good natured BS-ing, we started reminiscing about the guys we knew in 'Nam—you, Peter, the three Steves, Murphy, Ward, Marvin Miller and the rest. I forgot that he didn't know everybody since he was TDY with us off and on for four or five months."

Charlie paused. "Eventually, we both flashed back to that afternoon at the Continental Palace."

As soon as Charlie mentioned the words, my mind went off like a claymore, exploding with the most vivid images.

It was August, 1971. A hot, sticky day during the middle of the monsoon. About 11 a.m. or so, Charlie, Nevin, me, and Nevin's replacement at the First Air Cav paper, Marvin Miller, were sipping gin and tonics on the veranda of the beautiful Continental Palace in downtown Saigon.

We'd all been giddy from more than just the good booze. For the moment, we all believed that we were honest-to-goodness war correspondents, that we'd joined the ranks of Hemingway and Orwell—and even Halberstam and Sheehan.

Suddenly, Miller and Nevin launched into their Graham Greene routine, reciting passages from *The Quiet American*. According to them, Greene had written the book out there on that exact veranda nearly 20 years ago. A lot of the scenes in the book took place right there as well. I sipped my gin and tonic and smiled, amused by their playacting.

"But haven't you finished with him already, Pyle?" Nevin had asked, pretending to be Thomas Fowler.

"I can't," Miller had replied as Pyle, the "Quiet American." "In the long run, he's the only hope we have. If he came to power with our help we could rely on him."

"How many people have to die before you realize . . ."

"Realize what Thomas?"

"That there's no such thing as gratitude in politics."

"At least they won't hate us like they hate the French."

"Are you sure? Sometimes we have a kind of love for our enemies and sometimes we feel hatred for our friends."

"You talk like a European, Thomas. These people aren't complicated."

"Is that what you've learned in a few months? You'll be calling them childlike next."

"Well . . .in a way."

Nevin and Miller stopped acting. We shared a moment of silent reflection. Graham Greene had predicted what Vietnam would be like for us. We four were living proof of that.

Nevin had ordered another round to break the silence, but our group epiphany hung in the stale Saigon air, floating in our gin and tonics.

"Rick!" Charlie brought me back to the airport. "Are you following me?"

"Sure. I just can't help getting off on that day at the Continental Palace. We stayed there through the night, drinking and talking and singing and reciting poetry. It was one of the best fucking days of my life."

Both Charlie and I were struck by how serious I sounded. It was hard for us to believe that even one goddamn day in Vietnam had been good for anybody. It was one of those things we never talked about, that 'Nam had, in fact, been good for me. Unlike Charlie, I found myself in the Army. I belonged with guys like Nevin and Miller and the rest. Charlie belonged home with his family. For him, Vietnam was a uniform he'd worn for 365 days. When he got back, all he had to do was change his clothes.

"Anyway," Charlie continued. "Nevin and I are almost passed out and I causally say something like, 'Too bad about fucking Miller' or whatever and Nevin stops me cold. 'What about Miller?' he asks me.

'What do you mean what about Miller?' I shot back.

'What the fuck happened to him!' Nevin shouted, grabbing me by the shirt.

'Jesus Christ, Nevin,' I shoved him away. 'He's dead. Killed. In Vietnam. Official explanation: 'friendly fire.'"

"I'd never seen anything like it," Charlie spoke more slowly now, his voice barely audible against the arguing at the nearby table. "Nevin literally shrank before my eyes. He fell on the floor, shriveled up into a ball no bigger than a bunker sandbag, and started crying."

"You mean he didn't know?" I stupidly asked.

"What do you think?" Charlie snapped. "You figured he did. Hell, we all thought Nevin knew because it sure seemed as if he was behind our getting totally wasted the night we found out about Miller's death—the champagne toast, the dramatic reading of *The Quiet American*, the acapella version of 'Fortunate Son' at the top of our lungs.

"But Nevin wasn't there," Charlie's voice quieted. "Maybe his spirit was, but he'd DEROS-ed two days before Miller's 'accident.' Somehow he never found out. I sure as hell killed his fucking spirit by telling him about it that night."

"What did you do?" I couldn't believe what Charlie was telling me.

"This is the weird part," Charlie confessed, grabbing my wrist and staring me in the face. "I hit him."

"You what?"

"I hit him. I sucker punched one of my best friends. And I kept on hitting him. Over and over. God, I busted him up pretty bad."

Tears welled in both our eyes. I couldn't speak.

"I hit that little sonuvabitch and he whimpered. I hit him again and he cried. Then I kicked him and he just started whimpering. I grabbed stuff off the table and threw it at him. Hitting. Cursing. Kicking. Again and again and again."

I placed my hands over my ears and turned away. The Vietnamese at the next table were looking straight at me. What did they see? Did they know me from before? From back then?

"I left Nevin on the floor of that bar and never saw him again," Charlie went on. "I casually tell one of my closest pals that one of his friends was killed in Vietnam, killed by his own fucking self when he tripped and fired his own goddamn M-16 as he was going to take a shit—and then I beat the fucking daylights out of him."

"The Quiet Americans," I mumbled to myself.

"Do you know why I'm telling you this?" Charlie bullied me. "Do you understand why?"

I shook my head. The Vietnamese had stopped paying attention to us and were getting ready to leave.

"You're fucking clueless, aren't you?" Charlie snarled. "I'm telling you this because I slugged my priest the other day and took a swing at my wife, too. I can't stop."

I couldn't think of anything to say. I thought Charlie had everything worked out. If he didn't, where did that leave me?

"I've gotta catch a plane," I started to get up.

"Go ahead," Charlie mumbled.

"You wanna walk me to my gate?"

"Forget it," he waved me off. "I'm not leaving yet."

As we stood, the Vietnamese smiled in our direction.

"Fucking dinks," Charlie muttered. He sat back down and turned his back on them, and me.

* * *

I caught my plane to Chicago. That was almost a year ago. Before Cheryl. And the nightmares. And the uncontrollable weeping.

But I haven't called Charlie and talked to him about all this. We don't talk anymore.

Test Drive

"Where's the mutt?"

No response.

"Where in God's name is the mutt?" The question was noticeably louder this time.

"Say what?" a voice muttered.

"*Who in the hell took the mother fucking mutt?*"

Man, there was heat behind that question, and its incendiary source was Sergeant Carl Cassidy. Cassidy didn't just ask a question, he punched you with it.

There he was. Perfectly square shoulders, locked jaw, Popeye forearms, crew cut, penetrating eyes. Cassidy was the quintessential MP. And he had an air of Steve McQueen about him, the take-no-prisoners McQueen of *Wanted Dead or Alive* who dispensed his own brand of justice.

The mutt in question was our unit's M151 Jeep, its Army acronym identifying it as a "Military Unit Tactical Truck." Mutts were as Army as GI Joe and as American as Henry Ford. In fact, Ward had told us they'd been tested and prototyped by Ford and manufactured by the Willys-Overland Motor Company.

Ward also reminded us that whenever he drove a mutt in Vietnam, with its split windshield and horizontally-slotted, stamped-steel front grille, he felt like bursting into a chorus of "Fun, Fun, Fun."

And that's probably just what Ward was doing. He'd unofficially requisitioned the mutt for the weekly IO run to the PX for beer and cigarettes for the hooch and cognac for Bau Mau, and, more likely than not, a pit stop at Cholon for a quickie.

Cassidy, however, needed the mutt "A-SAP" as he reiterated in a voice that sounded like used sandpaper and suggested a belief that increased volume would cause the vehicle to materialize. Colonel Brock, it turned out, required immediate transportation to the squash courts for his late afternoon match.

No mutt. No Ward. No match.

Someone nervously started to whistle. Then another. Nevin added some quiet crooning. You could almost hear the voice of Frank Sinatra singing about an irresistible force, an immovable object, and that something had better give:

"Atten-hut," came a summons from the rear of the hooch. Footsteps scurried, zippers zipped, jungle boots replaced flip flops.

Colonel Brock strode into the IO hooch, sunglasses at 12 o'clock high.

"Gentlemen, I have some bad news. . ."

Confessions of a REMF

They called us REMFs, short for Rear Echelon Mother Fuckers. Sweet, isn't it? The "they" were the grunts, the GIs in the bush, the ones who humped the boonies and were in the shit.

That's how it was in Vietnam. Acronyms. Shorthand. Crudity. In your face. That's how it still is, too.

Sure, guys like me—there were some women too—were REMFs. Hell, all we did was fly and fix the choppers and the planes, drive the trucks, build the roads and the bridges, eavesdrop, interpret, supervise, and heal.

Some of us wrote the stories and some of the stories didn't get written and some of the truth never came out. That's the Vietnam I'm still dealing with. It makes me worse than a REMF. It makes me a fraud and a liar. It makes me responsible.

Now that the journalist Hersh has come out with the truth about My Lai, I feel like I have to tell my truth, too. It's not as horrible and huge as My Lai, but it eats me up. I'll bet if you added up all these little things from everybody's time in Vietnam, it could amount to a whole bunch of My Lais.

And who pays the price for all that guilt and shame? We do. The REMFs and the grunts do.

* * *

I started my tour seated in a windowless box in a remote radio compound somewhere near Cambodia. There was a black guy with me, Moore I think his name was, and we spent our shifts there, tuning a radio dial, headphones clamped on, secretly eavesdropping on enemy communications—ever vigilant, always hoping to intercept that one piece of intelligence that could make the difference in a battle or in the whole fucking war and let us all go back home where we belonged.

After a while, they gave me a new MOS and sent me down to Long Binh, near Saigon, where I pounded away on an ancient typewriter, edited a bunch of bullshit stories, and fought the unrelenting boredom. My bosses, and there were a bunch of them, kept reminding me to get a haircut and trim my mustache. They also explained that while I was performing a job that wasn't very glamorous, what I was doing was very, very necessary.

So what did I do that was so wrong? Besides being in the Army that is? Two things really. I copped out on letting a big, important story see the light of day.

And I turned my back on a fellow soldier because I was a coward and, well, somebody had to pay for my mistake. More or less in that order.

I still have a copy of the piece I wrote but was afraid to leak to a civilian reporter. I knew who to give it to and how and when to hand it off. His name was Sheridan and he wrote for *Newsday*. A bunch of us 71Q20s—that's military-speak for Army information specialist/journalist—had sneaked some stories to him over time, small shit mostly designed to give the lifers heartburn like the fancy bowling alley they were building for the brass at Long Binh or the extra bronze stars the Army was passing out like candy so all the career soldiers could get promoted.

We always worried about getting caught, but we trusted Sheridan—with the small stuff at least. Then why not give him the bigger stories, more access? Chickenshit I guess. Which is why I sit confessing this to you, and Sheridan is in jail somewhere for protecting his sources and some innocent people are dead. *Fuck me* is about all I can say.

It's time I owned up to the story I wrote back then about all the shit that was going down at what we affectionately referred to as LBJ. No, not the president. LBJ stood for Long Binh Jail. And if ever there was a hell on earth, it was LBJ.

* * *

DATELINE: Long Binh, South Vietnam—The anger of EMs imprisoned in Vietnam by the Army brass has finally exploded. Hundreds of GIs fed up with military oppression have rebelled at the Army's largest stockade at Long Binh, twelve miles north of Saigon.

Known as "LBJ," the U.S. Army Vietnam Installation Stockade (USARVIS) at Long Binh was the primary incarceration center in Vietnam. Designed to house the Army's malcontents and criminals, LBJ placed imprisoned GIs on a daily diet of lousy food, overcrowding, long delays before trial, and inhumane treatment.

Thus, when the Army introduced a new policy of strip-searching inmates in an effort to stem the proliferation of drugs, LBJ inmates took this as the ultimate act of degradation. And on the night of August 29, the lid blew. . . .

* * *

Jesus, no wonder this article never went anywhere. Even an Army lifer could have written a better lead. Get to the fucking point, GI!

Truth is, I didn't know that the point was, and if I did, I wouldn't know how to get to it. And who would give a flying fuck anyway? I was just another in a long line of Vietnam whiners, short on maturity and objectivity, grousing about the Army and Vietnam.

My other predicament was that this wasn't really my story since the brass wouldn't let us journalist types into LBJ until they had control of the situation. Which means I had another source for this scoop, an inside man, Specialist Four Billy Turner, who was new to LBJ and had a deep sense of right and wrong. What he saw that night bothered the shit out of him—which is why, I think, he brought his story to me.

So, the LBJ saga is actually Turner's story, as told by yours truly. But the bored, tired, and intimidated me forgot the old Sgt. Joe Friday rule of "changing the names to protect the innocent." Not that any of us are really innocent, but you get the picture. I fought the law and the law won, and I screwed Spec. 4 Turner in the process.

* * *

I can still see his bright eyes and tightly-clipped mustache. Everything Turner took in struck him as uniquely special, and when it didn't comply with his world view, he'd crinkle his forehead and let out a whistle, a sound that signaled "Man, this isn't right."

I met Turner on his first day in country. He'd just been assigned to Company A, 720th MP Battalion, 18th MP Brigade, and it took him forever to arrive at the Long

Binh compound. The minute he hit his cot, he was told to report to the unit armory. From there, Turner and his brothers-in-arms made a quick pit stop at the nearby mess, and that's where the Vietnam gods brought us together.

I was delivering the *Morning News Roundup*, our office's daily dose of propaganda—one page, front and back—that we delivered to the mess halls on post. I noticed Turner looking lost and forlorn. I gave him one of those "Newbie, I know the kind of bullshit you're dealing with" looks and handed him a copy of the *Roundup*.

"What's this?" Turner asked.

"All the news that's unfit to print," I shot back, smiling.

Some of the guys in line with Turner laughed, but he didn't get it.

"Did you ever hear the saying 'military justice is to justice as military music is to music'?" I asked Turner. He shook his head vigorously, so hard that you could almost hear all the noise inside.

"Think about it a minute," I paused, a slight look of recognition appearing on Turner's face. "It's the same with the news. We write what they tell us to write. So do most of the civilian reporters. It's not real, any of it, because the stuff we write and publish makes us look like heroes—kicking Charlie's ass, winning the hearts and minds of all the natives. Shit, as the Vietnamese themselves would say: 'Nevah happen, GI.'"

Turner let out one of his knowing whistles before he was hurried off to be outfitted with a flak jacket, a fully-loaded M-14—complete with an unsheathed bayonet, no less—tear gas, grenades, and a gas mask. Next thing you knew, he was on his way across the base to the notorious LBJ to quell an uprising by American GIs.

Five days later, Turner was standing next to my bunk, telling me his incredible story and begging me to write it all down. And to get it out.

"No matter what," he told me, his forehead doing that honesty crinkle, "no matter what, this story has to get out."

What Turner saw and experienced in those five days changed his life forever, and mine, too. But I'm rambling, probably because I'm afraid to keep going, to get to the nub of all this. Something inside me knows that my confession alone can't relieve all the fucking guilt and responsibility, that it won't save lives or turn back time.

Still, it's important to come clean, to seek absolution, if only from myself. It matters that somebody, some time realizes what the fuck we had to do over there and what we did to one another. Maybe it can help explain why things are so fucked up back here. That's what the LBJ "disturbance" epitomizes—a mini-drama on the big stage that was Vietnam, one that opens a window to the putrid air we had to suck into our lungs for 365 days.

Shit, we still can't exhale.

* * *

So, what was LBJ like? Our office had done some earlier stories about it, puff pieces mainly, the latest one pumping up the new light bird the Army brought in to run the place in July. I wrote that pile of shit, too. Vernon D. Johnson was his name. Arkansas born and bred.

Otherwise, our access to LBJ stories, especially LBJ prisoners, was totally off-limits. But even a fucking blind lizard could stumble upon an LBJ turd. Mind you, these were America's finest young men: guys who'd answered the call and took up arms, but were now branded as "inmates," spending their days in tedium and humiliation.

For those not inclined to follow the LBJ rules, there was the glorious "Silver City," the maximum confinement area made up of converted Conex shipping containers. I know for a fact—because we stored copies of our weekly Army newspaper in these things—that temps inside those boxes exceeded 120 degrees. Who can live like that? Nobody. No wonder imprisoned GIs saw this as a form of torture and why Silver City helped nail LBJ's reputation as the worst fucking place to be in 'Nam.

To top it off, just like my old neighborhood back home, you could cut the racial tension in this eight-acre compound with a government-issued can opener. The fucking overcrowding was the *coup de grâce*. When I interviewed Lt. Col Johnson he admitted that LBJ was designed to only hold about 400 inmates and the number had exceeded 700 and was still climbing. I was ordered not to put that in my article.

We knew the other numbers but never reported those either—that black GIs made up almost 90 percent of LBJ's inmate population, that they displayed their defiant identity with "Black Power" signs and intricate hand gestures, while the predominantly white—and racist—guards didn't have a clue how to deal with an angry, dapping GI with an Afro.

In short, LBJ had been a booby trap since it opened. But thanks to the Army's public relations campaign—

aided and abetted by lazy civilian journalists—most of
what went on at LBJ remained essentially quiet, despite
uprisings in 1966 and 1967.

* * *

There it is. By August 1968, (here's the best line from my
story) "the embers of the flames from the American
cities that had burned the previous two summers,
intensified by the April 1968 assassination of Martin
Luther King Jr., finally ignited the smoldering environ-
ment at the Long Binh Jail." Definitely Pulitzer caliber,
wouldn't you say?

The way the official story goes—and it's out there for
anybody to read—a small group of black "militants" got
high on drugs and attacked the LBJ fence guards in the
admin sector. From there, total chaos ensued as the
rebels burned mattresses, tents, and trash. Within
minutes, the mess hall, supply building, latrine, barber
shop, and administration and finance buildings were
ablaze.

Everybody not rioting was taken by surprise, especially the guards. Turner said that by the time the guards
realized what was happening, more than 200 prisoners
had joined in the riot, systematically destroying the
camp and beating guards and other white inmates with
wood planks and bars from dismantled beds.

Around midnight, Lt. Colonel Johnson and his aide-
de-camp entered the compound, expecting to calm the
rioters. While addressing the mob, Johnson was sucker
punched, kicked and pummeled, sustaining a major
head wound before he escaped.

By that time, Turner and the other MPs were helping
the prison guards shore up perimeter security, with a

platoon of fire trucks standing by. A significant number of those who'd opted not to join in the riot were escorted by the MPs to a secure field adjoining the prison where they waited out the night under close guard.

By now it was August 30. Turner and his unit were ordered to hustle to the stockade front gate and assemble in a V formation. He watched and waited.

"Every time the front gate opened," he told me, "we formed a barrier to follow whatever vehicle went in. We did this all day and all night."

By the 31st, the mood of LBJ prisoners, according to Turner, had swung from racial discord to revolt against the Army. In unison, black and white inmates threw rocks and debris at him and the other 720th MPs who were hunkered down on the outer perimeter. The smell of burning debris from the fires was so strong and pungent that Turner had to put on his gas mask.

Once the perimeter guard was established, the waiting game began. Turner said it felt like some heavy duty poker game, with the Army holding all the cards. They could just sit back and wait you out because they'd stacked the deck. Hell, they owned the whole fucking casino. Turner's hand was pretty shitty too, pulling 12-hour shifts, constantly being cursed at, and baited into approaching the fence.

"If you happened to venture too close," he admitted, "the inmates would spit or piss on you."

Later that evening, several truckloads of blankets, cots, and food were brought in for the prisoners. Turner and the MPs formed a skirmish line at bayonet point so the gates could be opened to get the trucks inside, unloaded, and removed. That was when everything fell apart for him.

"It was just too weird," Turner told me, whimpering, "too weird and too un-American to be holding a bayonet-tipped and loaded rifle pointed at a fellow soldier, a brother no less, knowing you'd have to kill him if he rushed you. I mean, why wasn't I pointing my weapon at Charlie?"

Turner never went back to his post at LBJ. He came looking for me.

Eventually, the number of holdouts dwindled to a dirty dozen, and by the end of the week, they surrendered too. Those sorry SOBs realized, I think, that anyone who didn't give up, or give in, would be charged with attempted escape. Trust me, nobody in 'Nam, not even these guys, wanted any more time added to their sentences, or to their tours.

Right around this time they let us media types in—notepads, microphones, and cameras even—to watch them mopping up. There was even an impromptu statement delivered by Col. Johnson (he'd been promoted and given a bronze star 'cause of being attacked). The colonel reported that while the LBJ disturbance had left 63 MPs and 52 inmates injured, "there was one lone fatality, a Private Edward Haskins of St. Petersburg, Florida, who was beaten to death with a shovel."

I couldn't help myself. Standing there in what looked like Watts or Newark, listening to this Army bullshit, something snapped. "What about the four that got away?" I burst out. Turner had told me about the four escapees, and I was sick and tired of all these pussy-ass journalists standing around and playing along as if this was just another installment of the five o'clock follies.

I didn't get to hear the rest of Col. Johnson's crap because I was immediately yanked out of line by a very big—and very pissed off—MP.

"You think this is your press conference, solder?" he snarled, forcing my left arm behind my back so far and so fast that my fingers were almost touching my ear. "These fucking scum bags killed a United States soldier, and you want everybody to know that some of them got away? I'm going to have to kick your sorry ass."

A freshly-scrubbed lieutenant jumped between me and the MP. He, too, looked unhappy, but he had his arm on the MP's shoulder, urging him to ease up. He turned back to me and was right in my face.

"What's your name, Specialist?"

"Spec. 4 Bailey, sir."

"Specialist Bailey, how the fuck do you know that four inmates escaped from the stockade?"

* * *

You know what comes next. I keep asking myself, why did I give up Turner? Was it the pain in my left arm? The look of pure hatred in the face of the MP? The fear of court-martial and being sent to the DMZ?

I kept remembering what Turner had said about poker and the Army holding all the cards, and in that moment before I started blurting out what I knew, I saw myself throwing down my hand, aces and eights, saw me being cleaned out by Col. Johnson and the faceless lieutenant and the pissed off MP. I knew I was screwed. And as soon as my survival instinct kicked in, Turner was toast.

The story I finally did get to write about LBJ focused on the 129 courts-martial that were levied against the "insurrectionists" for charges including murder, assault on a superior officer, aggravated assault, mutiny, aggravated arson, larceny, and "willful destruction of government property." It was a big story and it was juicy. It got me bumped up to Spec. 5.

The real irony of the LBJ riot was the lack of coverage it received in the mainstream media, despite the fact that the Army had given the story to so many members of the press. The Army's reports highlighted the fact that the riot was racially motivated and was patiently quelled. Unlike My Lai and a lot of other shit during the war, the 1968 riot at LBJ was a public relations tactical victory for the military.

* * *

So, go ahead and call me a REMF. I've been called worse. By myself even. Hell, I've lost count of all the names and faces and dates and places I fudged or chose to ignore. I'm trying not to remember the lives, the honest to goodness human lives, I maybe could have saved.

And then there are words. Words that I wrote and, even worse, those that I didn't. And those few I uttered that hot September day in 1968.

I was in a position to expose things, even if only to my own heart.

And I didn't.

I was a coward. I *am* a coward.

And now that I've told you my story, you're a part of it, too. You can pardon me, forgive me, or wag your finger at me and tell me I fucked up.

That's how it was in Vietnam. That's how it still is, too.

Moron Corps

"Goddamn, Hawk," muttered Arthur Poole as his city's infamous wind slapped him in the face and curled inside his pea coat. Arthur's sidekick, Lanny Watkins, quivered like a pool cue.

"Man, it's fucking c-c-c-cold!" The loquacious Lanny could hardly talk.

"What else is new?" Arthur deadpanned.

Both men scanned the line in front of them. It zigzagged along and up Michigan Avenue, its numbers of shivering brothers ebbing and flowing. Someone up ahead told them that yesterday's line was twice as long as this one.

"Shit, man, we'll freeze to death 'fore we get to the front of the goddamn line!" Lanny's teeth were chattering. "I have n-n-n-never in my life been so cold. Damn line ain't m-m-m-moved in an hour . . . what a s-s-s-sorry-ass d-d-d-deal this is . . ."

Arthur half-listened, figuring that Lanny was talking to keep himself warm.

"By the time we get to the front of this f-f-f-fucking line, Uncle Sam's gonna be out of j-j-j-jobs and out of money. She-e-e-it. . . . ."

Arthur gave Lanny a look that said shut up and kiss my ass simultaneously. Lanny stopped talking.

"Brother, you don't know shit," Arthur eventually broke the silence. "Them Army recruiters that come through Cabrini-Green the other day ain't goin' home empty handed. Like the sign says: Uncle Sam Wants You!—and me—and the rest of the brothers standing in this line."

Lanny was taking this in when the big dude in front of them turned around.

"You shoulda seen the badass that blew into Robert Taylor yesterday." The big guy lowered his head so that his words made their way down to Lanny and Arthur. "All shine and polish. Tight uniform. Lots of fancy medals. Big, booming voice. He told us if we joined up we'd get some schoolin' and be able to pick what Army job we wanted to do and where we wanted to go. Sure sounded sweet to me." The big guy smacked his lips.

"Did the dude ever mention Vietnam?" Arthur asked.

"Just to say that's where they send the draftees," the big man replied.

Lanny whistled. Arthur shook his head.

"This is my t-t-t-ticket outta here," Lanny smiled. "I stay around the projects any longer and I'm going out f-f-f-feet first."

Arthur and the big fella laughed. Then the three of them shivered. Arthur kept thinking about what Buster, his cousin who joined up and ended up in 'Nam, had warned him about the Army. "Don't believe their promises. Watch what you sign. Don't ever trust the white man, " Buster told him.

But this deal was different, Arthur argued with himself, *this here program had been blessed by the secretary of defense hisself.* Project 100,000 he'd called it. They didn't have to come into Mother Cabrini's backyard and seek him out. They were trying to help him. Shit, there were no fucking jobs here.

"Did you ever take the test?" The big guy was trying to get his attention.

"Say what?"

"Did you take the qualifying test? The Army test?"

"Nah, dude said I could take it later," Arthur replied, looking to Lanny for corroboration. Lanny was bumming a smoke from the guy standing behind them.

"The black recruiter told me it don't matter what you score on the test, you're in." The big guy smiled. "California, here I come!"

The Hawk stung their cheeks. Arthur tried burying himself deeper into his jacket. Glancing at the fancy shops and deluxe buildings, he couldn't believe he only lived a mile west of here. What did these people know of his life? His troubles? Ain't no work for a guy like him in there.

The line started, then stopped. Small, slow steps. Around the corner floated the sound of sweet harmonies. Arthur strained to make out the words from a familiar Chicago song, but the Hawk blew the song away before he could remember the words.

The Girls They Left Behind

Lieutenant Brian Miller left behind Karla Bennett, his grade school, middle school and high school sweetheart. The cutest girl at Most Blessed Sacrament, Karla played Mary to Brian's Joseph in the first grade nativity play, at which point they decreed that divine intervention had brought them together and nothing, not even a war, would tear them apart.

Sergeant Arthur Poole left behind his fiancée Martha Brown, "the finest piece of ass in Kansas City," as his good buddy Willie Brown once described her. Arthur knocked out Willie's two front teeth for his saying that, and Willie never talked any trash about Martha again.

Corporal Joe Hudak left behind Sally McBride, even though he didn't know it. Spirited, strong, independent girls like Sally always found him. Sally was out there, somewhere in the USA, and once he got "back to the World," Joe would find her.

Petty Officer Hector Colon left behind his wife Pilar and her six brothers and sisters, two dozen aunts and uncles and 37 cousins. Hector would have to get Pilar out of El Campo, Texas, if he ever wanted to talk to her without some family member around, interrupting or commenting.

Private First Class Billy Donovan didn't leave anybody behind, so he pretended his sister Linda was the girl back home—a confirmed fox—according to the guys in basic training who'd seen her picture. "Man, if the game ends up in a tie and you have to kiss your sister, then life is good," his bunkmate Tommy DeFelice told him on more than one occasion.

The girls they left behind wrote letters and sent care packages and longed to visit their men on R&R in Hawaii. They watched the nightly six o'clock news but covered their ears when the reporters started to talk about the number of U. S. casualties in Vietnam.

They worked at low-paying jobs and went to movies with their girlfriends and spent lots of time with their families. They gave dirty looks to the guys who came hanging around. They went to bed every night with a prayer for their man's safety on their lips.

They waited.

The men who came back home were not the same men the girls had given such tender goodbyes. Brian Miller left large parts of himself in Phu Bai where he'd stepped on a C-40 anti-personnel mine and lost both his legs. Arthur Poole complained about the treatment of black soldiers who were still second-class citizens after they got back to the States. Joe Hudak threw his medals at the White House and convinced himself he was a war criminal. Hector Colon was pissed off all the time because he couldn't land a decent job. Billy Donovan never really came back.

The girls they left behind had to pick up the pieces.

Karla Bennett became Mrs. Brian Miller and tried to get Brian to sing along to the songs on the radio just like he did before he left. She spent six days a week working at the local Safeway and when she wasn't at work, she was taking care of Brian. She wondered if she'd married Brian because she felt sorry for him.

Martha Poole tried helping Arthur find a job and made an honest effort to like the Vietnam vets he brought around all the time. She twisted the shiny bracelet on her left arm, a lucky charm her mother had given to her years ago, and with every twist, she told herself that Arthur would get back home from Vietnam.

Sally McBride eventually found Joe Hudak, but she lost him pretty soon after that. He seemed like the perfect guy at first, but when he got back from a D.C. protest, Joe stopped sleeping with her, or even touching her, for fear of contaminating Sally with his Vietnam transgressions. She was angry about Joe's avoidance and she was mad about the war and the government and the VA and everything else. She was debating when exactly to split.

Pilar Colon spent most of her time on the phone, talking to her family back in Texas. She and Hector had moved north to Kansas City and were having a hard time adjusting. Her mother and sisters gave her daily, long-distance advice and propped her up. Hector was unhappy about their big phone bills.

Linda Donovan gave up on connecting with her brother Billy, so she dated a lot of Vietnam vets and volunteered at the Kansas City Vets Center. Always a good listener, Linda had a knack for saying the right thing at the right time and making people feel comfortable, which was probably why she became a group leader at the Center.

The men who came home gave up on just about everything, including the girls they left behind. They quit their dead-end jobs and stopped going to the State Employment Service where by-the-rules VFW types scolded them with their eyes about their appearance and their attitudes.

They gave the VA the finger and coughed up the shit they inhaled from the Vietnam jungles.

They joined the VVAW but watched their backs during raucous meetings where guys conspired to kill Nixon and blow up the Pentagon.

They missed the "three hots and a cot" the Army had delivered them daily.

Or they missed the adrenaline rush and the opium highs.

They missed their buddies.

They cursed their lives.

The girls they left behind joined the same therapy group, but they didn't call it that. Their rap group met every Wednesday night for two hours. Inside a tiny room with dirty beige walls, castoff furniture, and one lone light bulb they bared their souls and cried and swore and hugged and hollered.

The rap group girls, as they called themselves, smoked cigarettes and drank Mountain Dew. They broke the ice with bean bag tosses and swapped stories about their men. They laughed when they wanted to cry and cried when they thought they would laugh.

Linda Donovan ended up needing the group more than the group needed her. Her brother Billy died in a high-speed car accident and his death left a hole in her heart. The other women gave her the time and the space to bandage that wound.

Martha Poole and Sally McBride almost came to blows, but they dropped their guards and forged a bond. They both liked Goetz beer and rummage sales. Karla Miller helped Pilar Colon shop at her Safeway on double-coupon days. Pilar made quesadillas for Karla and the rest of the group.

The girls they left behind begged the men who came home to talk to them about how they were feeling, to hold them tight in bed at night, to join them in their Wednesday rap group.

The men who came home didn't know what to say. They were still fighting the war.

The girls they left behind grew strong and at ease. They sang Aretha Franklin songs and harmonized on "Neither One of Us" by Gladys Knight and the Pips. They cooked and they cleaned and they worked and they believed.

They held their men's hands and they prayed to their god. The only people they told about their own pain were one another. And they only did that on Wednesday nights.

The girls they left behind were no longer girls. They were women. They were pillars of strength and rivers of wisdom. They were the North Star and the true compass.

And slowly, eventually, they brought their men back home. To stay.

Every Picture Tells a Story

His fascination had started out as a nuisance, a distraction. But as his time drew closer and the noose around his neck tightened, it had become more a matter of survival.

Today, it had grown into a full blown obsession. That's why he had waited all these weeks for the book to arrive, why he'd begged and pleaded with the librarian to order it in the first place. By now he was absolutely convinced that if he knew more about Vietnam and its history that he would find a way to survive. *Yes*, he told himself, *if I have a deeper understanding of what makes the Vietnamese tick, then maybe, just maybe, I won't come home in a box.*

So, finally, here it was. She was signing the book out for him. *Viet Nam Su Luoc* by Tran Trong Kim, published earlier this year. She was smiling, obviously proud of herself for her persistence and resolve. She reminded him a little of his Aunt Mae, what she probably looked like when she was younger and her body had shape and she even cared about sex.

Yes, here it was. Now his entire body shuddered in reflexive response as he stared at the inside title page. There it is. *Những bộ sử Việt nam - Diễn Đàn Hạt Nắng*. Jesus, what a fucking idiot! Why hadn't it occurred to him that the book would be written in Vietnamese? How completely stupid could he be?

His heart was in his throat and his head was pounding as if Jon Bonham was inside his head, banging away on "Good Times, Bad Times." Jesus, but these were bad times.

He was done for.

He followed his nose to the clammy, dark recesses of the old library, sat alone among the dusty shelves and forgotten tomes, and gingerly opened the book as if it were a booby trap. Slowly, ever so slowly, turning the pages of Tran Trong Kim's manuscript, he stared at the pictures.

The recorded history of the Vietnamese people was unfolding in front of his eyes, but he could only experience it through illustrations, colorful drawings, and faded photographs. Maybe Vietnam's history was made up of images, not words? But words were what he needed. Words were what reassured him. Words were his life.

There was one particular drawing that grabbed him and wouldn't let go. The bright colors jumped off the page, especially the gaudy yellow background that reminded him of the French's mustard he used to put on his hot dogs at baseball games. But even more arresting than the bright yellow was the image of a tall, proud Vietnamese woman astride a large, white, menacing elephant.

He had never seen anything quite like this before. The young woman looked pissed and defiant, a crown upon her head and snakes that looked like swords in each hand. Her gown was yellowish-brown with what looked like a green flak jacket over her chest. The elephant, too, was dressed in this off-yellow and green material, his left foot lifted off the ground as if he were marching and his head and eyes titled directly at the viewer, one of his sharp, pointed tusks almost jumping off the page to stab you in the heart.

He sat there bewildered. He tried thumbing through the rest of the book, but kept coming back to that same page, that stunning image. Who was the young woman? Why was she riding an elephant? Who was she fighting? What did it all represent?

And why did they both look like they wanted to kick the living shit out of him?

* * *

Eventually, the janitor found him there, asleep with the book open on his lap. The tall black man closed the book, lifted it from the white boy's lap, and placed it on top of his cleaning cart. The janitor gazed quizzically at the cover, immediately recognizing the language as Vietnamese because the accent marks over the letters looked exactly like those in the pictures his son, an MP at MACV headquarters in Saigon, sent home during his tour.

You Baby Ruth

Every day my mother tells me to stay away from the round-eye Americans. When she talks about them, her voice grows taut, much like the *day-thep gai*, barbed wire, the soldiers surround us with.

"*Nguoi My that xau*," she says to me, "American very bad."

I obey my mother but I am curious about the bad Americans.

Every night, after we bed down the water buffalo and prepare the *Nước chấm* and rice for the next morning, my grandmother tells me and my younger brothers and sisters about the Chinese, French, and Japanese who were here before the Americans. She speaks of great battles and heroes.

My favorite story is Trieu Au, a peasant girl like me, who launched a revolt against the Chinese nearly two thousand years ago, long before the Americans and the French. Trieu Au killed herself rather than surrender. My grandmother tells me her last words:

"I want to rail against the wind and tide, kill the whales in the sea, sweep the whole country to save the people from slavery."

At night, I go to sleep dreaming about wearing golden armor alongside Trieu Au as we ride elephants into battle against mighty whales. I look strong and mighty, and my sword is swift and silent, lopping off the flippers of the whales that dare rise up in our path.

* * *

My father is away fighting and my brothers and sisters
are too little to help with the harvest, so I rise before the
sun to fetch the water from the well. I move quickly like
a cat in my sandals made from the rope and rubber that
the Americans leave behind in junk heaps. I start a fire
in the cooking pit outside our hut and fill the pot with
rice. Then I go inside and wake my family—my mother,
grandmother, two brothers, and two sisters. I eat my
rice, grab the food my mother has packed for me, and
rush into the rice fields.

We can waste no time during the rice harvest. The
American soldiers are always bombing, digging up, or
spraying our fields. I strip down to my underwear and
go to work, using the sickle my grandmother sharpened
the night before. I like the feel of the mud between my
toes and the swishing sound the sickle makes as I cut
the heavy stalks of rice from their submerged roots. The
stalks are tough. The sickle must be sharp.

On my way home in the afternoon heat, I watch our
elderly neighbor Thanh fishing with a long bamboo
pole. He smiles at me and offers his biggest catch.

"*Cam on, ong gin,*" I thank him. My family will be
happy to have fresh fish.

I take the shortcut along the highway. My mother
has warned me about taking this way home, but it is
late. She will not be angry with me when she sees the
fish.

As I make my way among the puddles down to the
highway, I hear the roar of moving vehicles. A herd of
tanks, stampeding down the road, throws out mud and
noise. At the rear of the herd is a Jeep with three American soldiers. I shudder and try to run back the way I've
come, but they have seen me.

One of the soldiers salutes me and laughs. The second holds up his gun and pretends to shoot—"Bang! Bang! You dead gook." I jump to avoid his make-believe bullets. The third soldier, the one who is driving, stops the Jeep, gets out and walks over to where I am holding my hands against my ears. He places his hand on my shoulder—light and soft like a butterfly—and speaks softly in Vietnamese. I have never heard an American speak Vietnamese before and this one speaks very well.

"*Biệt sự sợ*, don't be afraid," he tells me. "GI numbah 10. You numbah one. I like Vietnamese."

His hands reassure me, but the two other soldiers in the Jeep shout at him, calling him *giao-sur* or professor and calling me "gook."

"*Giao-sur*," I address the nice American. The professor responds, and the two men burst out laughing and slap one another on the back.

The professor hands me a small candy bar in a white wrapper with big English letters.

"You Baby Ruth," the professor says to me, smiling and pointing to the letters. He walks back to the Jeep and waves goodbye. The two other soldiers keep laughing.

I arrive home very late, and my mother scolds me while my grandmother slaps me on the wrists. Not even the fish makes them happy. They send me to bed without any dinner. I lie awake listening to my mother and grandmother talking about the American soldiers they saw near our village. I clutch my Baby Ruth bar and think about the professor and then I am dreaming of Trieu Au, the two of us slaying one large whale after another.

* * *

The next morning, I awake early and leave for the rice fields in the dark. Before the sun is halfway across the sky, I hear the noise of tanks and trucks and see the dust moving along the highway. I return to my cutting, but there are two American soldiers walking through the puddles toward me. I stand still, holding my sickle beneath my shirt. As they move closer, I recognize the professor.

"*Chao co*," the professor greets me. I lower my head and return his hello.

The professor kneels in front of me and explains that he and his comrades are establishing a base camp down the road and will be coming to visit our village very soon. He says that he will bring presents to me and my family. They will teach us to speak English and learn more about his people and his country.

The man next to him, a large American with a small head and starched olive green pants that sparkle in the sun, says nothing. He looks around, shifting his weight back and forth from one leg to another, as he makes loud, squishing sounds in the mud.

That night I tell my mother about the nice professor who will soon be our neighbor. She holds her hands to her mouth, trembling. She makes me repeat my story to several villagers. My grandmother reminds them that it was like this years ago when the French were here. Now they are gone. Grandmother says the Americans will soon give up and our lives will be back to normal.

* * *

Two days later, the professor and his comrades arrive at our village. They drive up in a topless Jeep with dark

green and black swirls on the sides that remind me of
Trieu Au's whales. The professor speaks with the people
and he is especially kind to my grandmother. She
pinches me after the Americans leave and says: "*Nguoi
My nay lam tot.*" American is very good.

That evening, the people listen to the professor explain why he is here. The Americans will help us grow
more rice, prevent sickness, and protect ourselves
against the Viet Cong. His Vietnamese is very good.

Later, my grandmother tells the villagers to believe
what the professor says for now.

"*Giao-sur* reminds me of the ancient poet Nguyen
Trai," my grandmother observes, "'better to conquer
hearts than citadels.'"

* * *

The professor and his men return to our village every
day, bringing food in cans, needles with strong poison
fighters, cigarettes, weapons, and Baby Ruth candy.
Before long, the professor is teaching us to speak English. During the heavy monsoon rains and most of the
dry season, my mother lets me attend the lessons,
smiling as she recalls her French lessons when she was
a little girl.

I learn English quickly. It is harder to speak than to
understand. It is better this way since I grasp more of
what's being said than the Americans realize. All except
giao-sur who winks at me every time he explains a new
phrase.

* * *

Two monsoons pass and the professor still comes to our village every day. In that time many of his comrades have left Vietnam. Not *giao-sur*. He is always here.

Late yesterday, I heard him talking to a man we hadn't seen, a water buffalo-like man he called Captain John's-zone. It frightened me. When I got home, I repeated the meeting in my head, trying to translate as I watched and remembered.

The water buffalo captain was asking *giao-sur* questions without waiting for answers. He spoke a lot with his hands and his cap, which moved back and forth.

When he had a chance to talk, the professor talked faster than normal, telling the captain how what he was doing was good for the Army's mission in Vietnam. But the captain wasn't listening. Eventually, he held up his hand for *giao-sur* to stop.

"That's all fine, Lieutenant," the water buffalo said, "but it doesn't explain why you stay on here, does it?"

"No, sir," *giao-sur* said. His voice was the one I use with my elders.

"Then why?"

"Well," the professor hesitated, "it's . . . it's the people."

"Speak up, Lieutenant!"

"It's because of the people, sir."

The captain seemed puzzled. "What people?"

"The Vietnamese," *giao-sur* said softly, like he was saying he was sorry. "I like and admire the Vietnamese people."

The captain waited. After a long pause the professor continued. "I love the language. And the country."

"For two years?"

"Yes, sir." The professor's face was red and his voice was warm with anger.

The water buffalo leaned over the professor as if he were going to bite his head. He shouted and barked and said something about me that I couldn't understand.

"Listen to me, Lieutenant, and listen good. Your job is to execute Army policy. Period. Win the hearts and minds of these stupid slopes and stop acting like one of them. Have I made myself clear? Follow orders and do as you're told."

The captain paused, leaning on the hood of his Jeep. "I hear they call you 'the professor.' Why is that, lieutenant?"

The professor would not speak.

"My guess it's because of all this teaching you're doing. Well, no more teaching. You read me professor? If I get one more report of your messing with our village programs, I'll cancel your extended tour and send you packing. You got me, Lieutenant? No more professor!"

"Yes, sir."

"That's all, Lieutenant. Dismissed."

Giao-sur saluted the captain, turned on his heels and walked slowly away. I didn't like the way the captain spoke to the professor. And I didn't like the way the professor had turned into a scolded child. I would tell him about Trieu Au.

* * *

I am walking back to my village from the rice fields when the professor drives up to meet me. I can't take my eyes off the black and green markings on the sides of the Jeep. The professor told me they are used for camouflage but I believe they're whales in disguise.

"*Toi tiec,* I am sorry," says the professor, his eyes pleading with me to join him. I get in the Jeep.

He drives into the countryside. I have never traveled beyond these fields. The highway passes over kilometers of rice fields laid out in perfect squares, separated by slender green lines of grassy, paddy-dikes and irrigation ditches filled with dirty water. The villages we pass are set far apart. Clustered around them are pockets of tiny huts, marking the hamlets where we have farmed since Trieu Au's time. I am part of one long rice paddy that stretches from China to the Mekong Delta and beyond, from the time of Trieu Au to the days of my great grand-children.

The professor talks as he drives, like he doesn't re-member I'm there.

"It's usually more difficult with the younger ones." He is talking about his argument with the water buffalo captain. "They're always the least sympathetic or sensi-tive. For them it's all cut and dried—you extend your tour in Vietnam because you want to get out of the Army early or because you like to hoard the tax-free combat pay you're making or . . . " He pauses and looks in my direction, "or else you're in love with a Vietnamese princess."

I don't have any idea, so I stare at the greens and wet browns of the countryside while he goes on.

"Their notions about loyalty are uncivilized. They only know the adolescent loyalty the army pounds into their heads during basic training." He gestures toward the rice paddies with his large, bony hands. "But I'm talking about a concept of loyalty that pertains to a mission and a people—one that goes beyond all that. Our job here is to make a better life for you." He waves a finger in my direction. "Just as my grandparents made America a better place for my parents and they made it better for me."

Suddenly, the professor sees something ahead that makes him pull off to the side of the road. We narrowly miss hitting an old man and his water buffalo as we bounce and slosh into a paddy dike. The professor leans over and pushes my head down, underneath the seat. He's breathing heavily and sweat pours down his cheeks. I hear the sound of large, heavy vehicles moving along the highway. Then a long silence.

"What's that you got there professor?" A sharp, high-pitched voice asks. "You got some jail bait under your seat, my man?"

For the first time since I've known him the professor cannot speak. Then he bends down and gently grabs me by the shoulders, lifting me to a sitting position. Standing in front of the Jeep is a large black soldier, with a broad, toothy smile on his face.

"Oooooo-weee!" the soldier squeals. "The professor done got his self some young putang." The soldier makes a smacking sound with his lips and slaps the professor across the back.

After a few minutes, the professor turns to me and says, very softly.

"*Toi tiec.*"

He gets out of the Jeep and walks the black soldier toward the highway. I listen to the distant sound of heavy traffic pounding down the highway. After a long time the professor returns to the Jeep, his face heavy with fear. He does not say a word as he drives me to my village.

By the time we arrive my family is standing in front of the cooking pit. They look frightened. My grandmother gives the professor a cold, harsh look as he helps me out of the Jeep.

"*Toi tiec,*" he says to her, removing his hat and half-bowing.

My mother and grandmother squeeze my hand. They send me and my brothers and sisters into our hut, and we hear them shouting at the professor. He keeps repeating "*Toi tiec.*" After a few minutes he gets back into the Jeep and drives away. I can hear him sobbing.

That night my mother puts my brothers and sisters to bed while my grandmother sits beside me by the cooking pit. I answer her questions about this afternoon, and she tells me that the American leader, the water buffalo Captain Johnstone, had come here this morning looking for the professor. Our neighbor told the captain that the professor had taken me for a ride in his Jeep. My grandmother believes me when I say the professor did not hurt me, but she is worried about what the Captain will do to him.

* * *

The American base continues to grow and grow, and soon there is fighting every night. Nothing happens during the day, but the Americans come here every morning to prevent us from meeting together. The soldiers look different now—they carry lots of weapons, they do not smile, and their fingers are pressed to their guns.

No one has seen the professor since the day of our Jeep ride. And then, this afternoon, he appeared, looking very tired. He summoned the head of every family to the square.

When our time comes, my grandmother goes alone. When she returns, my grandmother's face looks like ash. She tells us that there have been nighttime attacks on the American base, and the soldiers think our village is the source of the trouble. Captain Johnstone is convinced that there are Viet Cong in our village. He's ordering the professor to take suspected sympathizers back to the base so they will tell him who the enemy is.

* * *

One by one, hour by hour, day by day, the villagers go and come back. Most return quickly. Our neighbor, Tam Dong, is back in the fields by mid-morning, and his sons are beside him by noon. But my grandmother is kept the entire afternoon and she must return to the base the next morning.

That night, before I fall asleep, I listen to my grandmother telling my mother about her fears. Her voice sounds old and distant as she recounts the shouting, name-calling, and threats she endured for five hours. Even the professor was mean, although she says there were tears in his eyes.

I am awake the next morning when grandmother rises, waiting for her by the fire pit. I know that she will sharpen my sickle before she goes back to the base.

I watch her in silence. Her hands hold the sickle as if she is nursing a newborn. Carefully, she sharpens the blade on the stone until it shines brightly in the reflection of the firelight.

Grandmother comes over to where I am standing in the darkness. She hands me the sickle, whispering softly.

"Save our people from slavery."

As I turn toward the rice fields, I am surprised to feel my grandmother's arms tightly around my neck. She kisses my cheeks, my eyes, my ears, and neck. Then she places her finger to my lips and speaks quietly.

"Try and save the professor, too. He has forgotten the language that his heart is speaking. You must help him."

I hug my grandmother and walk into the darkness.

Later, when the noise first fills my ears, I think it is coming from the ground under the water in the rice fields. It sounds wet and hollow, then becomes louder and louder. I put my hands to my ears to try to mask the noise. Then I realize I am hearing the pounding of my blood. It is the sound of a broken heart, of a missing link. It is the sound of my grandmother's death.

* * *

We buried my grandmother this morning. My mother is still out at the gravesite, wailing to the night. I came back and put my brothers and sisters to bed and sat by the fire to look for answers. The oranges and luminous yellows tell of fires that destroyed my ancestors' homes. The smoke that drifts skyward from the fire is shaped like the elephant Trieu Au rode into battle against the Chinese. I fall sleep with that vision in my head as I hold my weeping mother in my arms.

* * *

I awake early, prepare my family's food, and walk toward the fields. But instead of going to work, I make my way to my grandmother's grave. I know that the professor will be there.

His back is toward me. I almost say something, then I stop and listen to the Vietnamese prayer he recites above her grave. His words are soft and soothing. His tears drip down his angular cheeks and make little pools of mud next to his combat boots.

I want the professor to turn around and look at me. I want him to see the elephant that I am riding.

I step toward the professor, the sickle above my head, and he begins to turn. I bring it across the back of his neck, my cut smooth and clean. There is a smile on his face as his head tumbles onto my grandmother's grave.

As I wipe the dark red blood off the sickle with my hand, I hear the waves crashing and the wind rising across the fields.

"I will rail against the wind and tide," I recite, *"kill the whales in the sea, sweep the whole country to save the people from slavery."*

Acknowledgments

With all due respect to Charles Dickens, Vietnam was the worst of the best of times and the best of the worst of times. The best of Vietnam resided in the men and women I served alongside (and those who preceded and followed me). Their friendship, resilience, courage, and good humor helped make the best of a horrendous situation. In the process, they helped me to cope with my 365 days "in country." I wish I could thank them all individually now, and wish like hell I'd thanked them back then.

The worst was what it was—an unpopular, unwinnable (from my vantage point), unforgiving war that sucked the life out of us, our families, and our country. America hasn't been the same since Vietnam, and probably never will recover, unless we confront everything that it did to us, especially the us who surrendered the best of our youth to the war's perpetration.

Yet the best and the worst and everything in between can never be erased from our memories. My year in Vietnam irrevocably changed me and my life. There isn't a day that goes by where I don't reflect on that place, those people—us and them—that time and those experiences. And the only way I've ever been able to make any "sense" of it, if there is any sense to be made, is to write about it.

I kept a journal the entire 365 days I served in Vietnam, wrote some bad GI poetry when I got back, focused my post-Vietnam graduate studies in English on the war, and have kept on writing ever since. At first, the writing primarily served as therapy, but after a while, when I couldn't quite get my Vietnam novel going but the urge to write kept gnawing at me, I wrote a very short story about my Vietnam experience. It was tight and tiny, only about 500-600 words, and later became the basis for the story "Malaria" in this collection. I got up the courage to share it with a published author, a wonderful Wisconsin fellow named Norbert Blei, and he didn't hate it.

So I wrote another story. And another. And I started inventing characters and then the characters started taking the stories where they wanted them to go.

I was learning how to be a writer.

I rewrote those first three stories for close to 20 years until I realized there was more to say about the experience of support troops in Vietnam. I drew on the men I knew, the assignments I completed in the field, and the stories I heard both there and back here. I read and re-read Hemingway's brilliant World War I collection *In Our Time* and used that as my North Star. I'm still trying—with the longer pieces as well as the interlinear mini-chapters—to reach Hemingway's height but know now that I'll always be reaching.

Finally, I benefitted from an extraordinary team of coaches, most of them Vietnam vets, through the Deadly Writers Patrol writing group. I don't know where DEROS would be without the guidance and support of Tom Deits, Tom Helgeson, Steve Piotrowski, Bruce Meredith, Wyl Schuth, Howard Sherpe, and Craig Werner. Thanks to the group's rigor – you had to prepare something to read every week—and constructive feedback, I was able to assemble the collection. With the help of Bill Christofferson, I found the talented folks at Warriors Publishing Group.

Yes, I'm one of the lucky ones—I went over and came back intact; I've had a good marriage, a great family, a fulfilling career, and supportive friends and communities. I thank them all.

But I'm especially mindful of those who never came back, not just the 58,195 on the Wall, but the hundreds of thousands who never got a hug or a hello or a thank you or an offer of help after they returned. Those are lives we should have saved, could have saved.

And to them I want to lead the nation in reciting the words: "We're sorry."

Doug Bradley
Madison, WI
Summer 2012

About the Author

Doug Bradley is a Madison, Wisconsin-based Vietnam veteran who has written extensively about his Vietnam and post-Vietnam experiences. He also has more than 30 years of experience as a communications professional in higher education, principally with the University of Wisconsin.

A native of Philadelphia, Pennsylvania, Doug earned his Bachelor of Arts in English from Bethany College. He also holds a Masters in English from Washington State University.

Photo by Jim Gill

Doug was drafted into the U. S. Army in March 1970 and served as an information specialist (journalist) at the Army Hometown News Center in Kansas City, Missouri, and U. S. Army Republic of Vietnam (USARV) headquarters near Saigon. Following his discharge and tenure in graduate school, Doug relocated to Madison where he helped establish Vets House, a storefront, community-based service center for Vietnam era veterans.

In addition to writing a blog for the *Huffington Post*, Doug is the co-author of *We Gotta Get Out of This Place: Music and the Vietnam Experience* with Dr. Craig Werner, UW-Madison Professor of Afro-American Studies, with an anticipated publication in 2013. The two also co-teach a popular course at UW-Madison entitled The Vietnam Era: Music, Media, and Mayhem.

Doug and his wife, Pam Shannon, are the parents of two adult children. *DEROS Vietnam* is his first book.